## The Symbolism of Ten

*Number ten stands for completion and achievement; it symbolizes the end of a circle and the expectation of a new beginning. When you add its two digits, one plus zero, you get one, the unit that symbolizes unity, force, power, divinity. It also represents loneliness. So the decagram, the ten-point-star, seals the end of the traditional world and is ready to shine on the downing new and hopefully better and more humane world, where people will not be isolated anymore.*

## About the Author

Catherine Pavlou was born in Athens, Greece in 1960. She studied public and European law in the University of Lille in France and she obtained her Master's degree and her Ph.D. from the University of Perpignan, France. Her career covers a wide range of occupations – and a long span of time – from office clerk to general manager and from probate lawyer to the current position of assistant professor in constitutional and public law. She has traveled quite a lot but she still lives in Athens where she teaches English, French and Greek.

# IN THE BEGINNING THERE WAS "X"

by Catherine Pavlou

Published 2006 by arima publishing

www.arimapublishing.com

ISBN 1 84549 121 1

© Catherine Pavlou 2006

Registered for copyright in the USA in 2005

Printed and bound in the United Kingdom

Typeset in Garamond 11/14

Swirl is an imprint of arima publishing.

arima publishing
ASK House, Northgate Avenue
Bury St Edmunds, Suffolk IP32 6BB
t: (+44) 01284 700321

www.arimapublishing.com

TO MY SON NICOLAS

## Acknowledgements

Special thanks are due to the team in Arima publishing and particularly to Les Gardner who had the patience to go through the text and correct all errors – although any mistakes are completely my responsibility – to Victoria Baldree for her terrific job on the cover design and to Lara Doran who guided carefully our collaboration. Furthermore I would like to thank those of my friends who stood by me and encouraged me to go on with this book. Last but not least, I thank my friend of friends and associate in past and future projects, Dimitris Myroyannis.

# CONTENTS

## Author's note

This book is not, and does not aspire to become, the feminist manifesto, or an anathema to homosexuality. It is a simple hymn to the old classic way of life: a boy and a girl, a man and a woman. You might answer to that that where there is love there follows pain, where there is marriage there is divorce. The old song: "love hurts, love scars, love wounds and mars every heart"[1] will lend support to your argument. So what? When you come to think of it, life is a huge risk, you never know what lies ahead; where there is pain, there is also – eventually – relief. Why stick to the pain that love inflicts on people when it ends and not to the wonderful moments – hopefully years – that it brings about while it lasts! And what happened once, may very well happen again and again. So why give up on traditional love, and not try to make the most of it?

This book is the natural consequence of the observation of the chromosomes layout in the human cell. Watching the phenomena, writing down the facts and going back to the – up to the moment known – history of man, certain conclusions emerged. I believe it is worth sharing them with those who would willingly ponder the question of the course of humankind, taking into consideration that every course has a beginning, and usually, an end. However, it is up to the *"dramatis personae"* (in our case the human beings) to determine if its course will end, and in what way.

The inspiration was totally unexpected and came up by chance, while searching in the Internet to find some information about chromosomes in general. For reasons of encyclopedic curiosity, all relevant pages found were searched, until I came upon the cell formation. It was hard to believe in my eyes. I had to read the same text a couple of times, in order to make sure that I was not dreaming it up. So, according to the author –

---

[1] BRYANT, Bordleaux. *"Love Hurts."* Lyrics. Perf. THE EVERLY BROTHERS. A Date with The Everly Brothers. Warner Brothers, 1960.

scientist, the female gene consists of two identical chromosomes, of two X, and it is symbolized by XX. On the other hand, the male gene consists of two different chromosomes, one X and one Y, and is represented by the letters XY.

It was the apocalypse! It was only logical to suppose that the male gene is half female, hence a variation of the female gene or even a genetic mutation, or a kind of evolution of the female. Therefore, female preceded male.

I do not intend to use biology or genetics jargon, as I am neither a biologist nor a genetics researcher. I will only try to retrace the mental associations that led to the conclusions mentioned above, based on the legal reasoning that resulted from studies in law.

First argument, the *de facto* numerical superiority of the chromosome X in relation to Y. If we presume that men and women exist in almost equal numbers – in order to keep things simple – on earth, this means that chromosome X is the 75% and the Y the 25% of the total of human sexual chromosomes.

Secondly, where there is a homogenous gene, the XX, and a heterogeneous, the XY, which is half female, we cannot rule out the possibility that Y came later, that it is more recent. It is quite possible that the evolution of the human species imposed the existence of Y, in other words a mutation of half of X, as necessary for the survival of humankind.

Finally, the male gene's name as XY sees that …ladies come first, both in Latin and Hellenic alphabets: either in the XY couple of letters, or in the XΨ couple of Hellenic letters, X comes first. Probably this cannot be attributed to a matter of simple courtesy towards women. Unless it was the X chromosome that was first located and studied.

Before the reader goes any further, I think it is time to clarify that as a human being, I do not suffer from inferiority or superiority complexes – two aspects of the same problem – towards men. In my system of beliefs, there are only people, good and bad, men and women, all necessary for life. The element of subjectivity that resides in the use of these nouns and adjectives has been fully taken into consideration. In no way shall I try to "prove" that men are an inferior or a lesser sex. Enough with this primordial discrimination that divided humans into men and second-rate citizens and that brought so many evils upon the world. Why perpetuate this discrimination, even if it be reversed?

The target is to make as clear as possible the fact that as a species, we have come of age, as we have been living on this middle-aged planet for thousands of years. Therefore, it is now time to leave all competition between men and women behind, even if this means to overcome the boundaries nature imposed on us. Let us keep in mind that nature's only preoccupation is the survival of the species it has created. It is high time both sexes ascended to higher spheres, together, because men and women can and must do it.

It is evident that this book is not a scientific treatise on the origins and the evolution of the species, or the superiority of the one or the other sex, but the depiction of the world seen from another point of view, seen chronologically from the eyes of a jurist, who looks for an answer to every question. Or, in order to use a favorite phrase among the youth, "to provide a problem for every answer". Apparently, it refers to those who are content and to those who seek to please.

All these thoughts and revelations and conclusions were in desperate need of some sort of order. They have also been clamoring to leave the shelter of my head and come out to the light. So I finally took the plunge and put everything in black and white, hoping that the reader will bear with me, and even if his or her patience results in conclusions different from mine, at least we will have travelled together and puzzled over the same questions.

# Year 125.897
# Safeland

It is a sunny morning, as always. No fog, no smog, no wind and no rain disrupt life in Safeland. Ever. Puffy white clouds chase each other playfully on the azure sky. The birds and the cicadas are not chirping however, as there are no more birds and cicadas on earth. Actually birds and 99% of the animal species have been erased from the planet thousands of years ago. Only memory activating material, like ancient books, films and CDs hold their images, for those few who still care. Cats, dogs, horses, fish and poultry, cattle, and wild beasts as well such as tigers, lions, hyenas, the colossal elephant and the tiny but lethal tarantula, are long gone. Even cockroaches, reputed to survive all catastrophes, had long exited this world.

Sadly, the huge majority of the Safelanders have been ignoring their natural history for generations. As for the history of the human race, they have no knowledge whatsoever. "We do not need this information", decree the administrators as often as they get the chance. "The past cannot be undone, let us think of the present, and of course of the future. We assure you, citizens of our safe land, that the objective of all our efforts will be more safety. This is the only conclusion that our foremothers bequeathed to us, that safety will never be enough. Do not forget, citizens, our worst enemy is the aggressive male. Do not listen to what they tell you, that the enemy lies within you. It is him who makes unholy desires burn in your chest (and belly), and then makes you feel guilty about it. He has been extremely canny, but, unfortunately for him, not canny enough to avoid his own demise. Always forward, Safelanders, to more safety". Sadly for them, they are unaware of the fact that nations that ignore their past have no future.

Masculina shakes her head to clear it from this monotonous, useless and senseless sermon. She lies down in her rocking chair, salvaged from the large heaps of relics from past eras, that remain forgotten in the city's warehouses, and takes her book – another relic of the same origin – on her lap. Contrary to her habit, she starts from the start. She is among the very few of her contemporaries who want to know. She does not want to dwell on what makes her special, not again. For the time being, she is ready to lose herself in the dawn of time.

\* \* \*

# FROM LILITH
*Year 125.897, Safeland*

When life was young on our planet earth, reproduction was assured by the simplest – and less messy – way, parthenogenesis. With an imagination that runs wild, we presume that in the beginning there were only amoebae, a single, asexual species, the X. Gradually, nature became playful, a little variety seemed necessary, maybe simply for experimental reasons, thus the XX came to life. However, parthenogenesis was no fun, it provided no grounds for acquaintances and developments, things remained permanently prosaic. It took nature a long time to realize that the reproductive way it had chosen was not fanciful to the contrary it was counterproductive. The decision was taken: a new gender would see the light of day, the XY, based on the already existing material XX. What was important was that the two beings would not be radically different from each other, a similarity due to a common origin would assure a degree of interaction, relations would emerge, actions and reactions would make the world a livelier place. Little by little, XX and XY – the salt of the earth – really made the world a more interesting place.

Let our imagination carry us back to the primitive women. The only objective in their lives was to give birth to new women. Nothing else mattered. Their muscular structure was feeble enough compared to the other inhabitants of the earth, the, always female, carnivorous and ferocious animals. Another problem they had to face in their every day routine was food. Burdened with babies, in their arms or inside their bodies, it was difficult to hunt. Last but not least, there was an endless monotony – I am to become this dinosaur's dinner, I eluded him, oh, there comes another one – which is in itself a lethal depressant. So there came a time when the need for another being, a stronger, more resilient creature, became pressing. This is how XY was designed and came to be born.

Gifted with sexual urge, intense aggressiveness and physically stronger than woman, man brought rapidly radical changes in the ways woman functioned and generally in her life. Soon XX and XY discovered the joys of sexual intercourse. However, the notion of family had not been conceived yet. The reason, or rather one of the reasons offered by researchers, is that man remained unaware for a very long time of his contribution in the conception of another human being. However, we do not agree with this version. In our opinion, all creatures on earth, since they became male and female, know by instinct that when they mate, their little ones will appear later. When, for example, the lioness seeks the lion to mate, and when he responds, in their lion minds they both know that the arrival of their cubs is imminent. Therefore we cannot accept that XX and XY were not aware, even on a primitive level, of their mutual share in procreation. Most probably, the current opinion is due to the myth of the woman-liar, who deceives man the gullible and naïve and trusting. This myth repeats itself through time and through religions, as we will see further on.

Let us stick for a while with this version - that of ignorance, maybe artfully cultivated by scheming woman. We can easily imagine that woman the mother was looked upon with awe, and maybe jealousy, by man the hunter and food-bearer. XY was with maintaining life, he was responsible for the survival, be it in the form of clan or tribe, but it was woman who held life in her absolute power. In a way, his role was auxiliary compared to the role of woman.

It sounds quite ideal, but also quite dull, to us, men and women of the 27th century, with our computers, our plasma T.V. screens, our D.V.D., our cars, the airplanes, space travel, our mobile phones and our minimum of 150 years of healthy life expectancy. But for them, there was never a

4

dull moment, what with the many savage animals that saw humans as their next meal, while storms, floods, earthquakes, lightning setting the forests on fire, made things harder. There were so many battles to fight, so many mysteries to solve, and later, so many gods to propiciate and gain their grace. Primitive people had no time to be bored, on the contrary, if they managed to survive, they aged rapidly and their life expectancy was very short.

The woman of that time, a primary being, created the matriarchal society, the core of which was life giving (birth) and life preserving (nurturing). In other words, the perpetuation of the species. Not much has been saved from this far-away era, however we may surmise that matriarchal societies were characterized by the system of joint ownership both of goods and children, which means that no individual father was assigned. Such societies, focused on life, can be mostly peaceful, arms were borne either for hunting or for defense.

Having seen the position of woman in the material primitive world, it would be enlightening to see what is the corresponding position of goddesses in the pantheon.

Moon must have been the first female deity worshipped by women, as the lunar cycle has always been thought of as the cause, or rather the origin, of menstrual cycle, thus the regulator of ovulation, the giver of fertility. For practical reasons, moon has also been the protector of the hunter, thus the giver of sustenance. So, moon was a goddess of a common utility, both to men and women. As a result, she has been considered harmless and left alone by men, when their kingdom came. However, other deities, exclusive to women, have not been so lucky.

Let us take the case of Lilith. Most scriptures scholars agree that up to the 7th century B.C. all Jewish religions were women-centered, hence their society must have been matriarchal. One of the goddesses was Lilith.

Until 625 B.C. when king Josiah imposed the rule of the male, and ordered the revision of all scriptures, and so all goddesses were erased (we can see how far back in time the roots of the "exterminator" go). However, Lilith remained in the oral tradition, not as a goddess any more, but as a female demon.

Actually, scholars disagree as to her real origin. Some say, as we saw above, that she was a Jewish goddess turned demon, others maintain that she was among the Assyrian and Babylonian religious deities, bequeathed to the Jews during their stay in Babylon. There are also those who insist that her name means "goddess" in Babylonian. One way or the other, she has been handed down the ages as the one responsible for the death-in-the-crib syndrome and also for the death of women during childbirth. As a protection against her evil, before labour pains begun, the midwives would nail on the wall above the mother-to-be an inscription that read, "be gone from us, Lilith". The inscription had to remain in place for months after birth above the crib, to insure the survival of the newborn. Another aspect of the folklore regarding this central figure in Jewish tradition, was also that of an evil night spirit who seduced men who slept alone. She would take their souls or /and she would drink their blood. From this point of view, she is the explication of men's wet dreams, who wake up in the morning spent but unsatisfied.

Her only appearance in the Old Testament can be found in the book of Genesis (Isaiah, 34:14): "Lilith (Lilit in Hebrew, meaning for some 'screeching owl', for others 'night breeze') will find the peace she deserves in the desert, with all the evil spirits like her". However, one cannot exclude the possibility that the good prophet was referring to owls or night winds.

Christians came, and gradually Lilith slipped into oblivion. Another deity took her place, Mary the mother of Christ and women turned to her for comfort. When, out of the blue, during the 11th century, a book titled

"The Alphabet of Ben Sira", whose writer was of Persian or Arabic origin, appeared. In this book of ambiguous conclusions but very clear intentions, we find a successful justification for the demonisation of Lilith. The forgotten fallen angel is presented as the first wife of Adam. The author goes on to explain that she was made at the same time as Adam and from the same materials, clay and divine breath. As a result, she was the same as Adam and she did not take kindly to his aspirations of leadership. Quite the contrary, she wanted to play leader, even in sex. She implored God to rid her from this despotic mate who demanded submissiveness from her part. But to no avail, God was a man too and turned a deaf ear. Frustrated and full of wrath, she evoked the name of God in vain, for the last time, and fled the Garden of Eden. She flew to the desert, where she met with the demons of her desolate soul, and mated with them. Her offspring were demons, condemned by God to die nightly in the hundreds, as punishment of her lack of obedience and respect and for her refusal to return and resume her God-assigned place.

Her former attributes of baby-killer and lone men-seductress came back, reinforced by Christian wrath.

In quiet a different context, Lilith appears in the Gilgamesh epic, as an always-laughing maiden, a mostly benign spirit, who lives in the Huluppu tree. The serpent has made his nest in the roots of this tree and Inanna, sister of Gilgamesh, cries her heart out and wants the residents (were they the first squatters?) thrown out. In this context, she could be assimilated to the Hellenic dryads, the goddesses who protected trees.

Finally, there are some theories according to which Lilith is related to Lamia, the legendary man-eater monster of Hellenic mythology, and to Hecate, goddess of the nether world and of black magic[2]. Especially after

---

[2] All the information about Lilith contained in this piece of work, come from the web site "alt.mythology" (www.lilitu.com), compiled by M. Barnard, (barnard@io.org)

the circulation of the book by Ben Sira, Lilith found her appropriate place in Jewish tradition: she was transposed in the Cabala.

Ever since, neo-paganists, mystic lovers, Satanists and feminists have all made a banner for their cause out of the myth of Lilith.

# TO ADAM

What could the objective of this tale have been? In our personal opinion, the objective must have been at least double: In the first place, the myth of the fallen wife was concocted in order to justify an early and hurried misinterpretation of the book of Genesis. The holy fathers, when they came upon the lines that God "male and female created them", hastened to construe that the two creatures were made simultaneously and from the same material, therefore equal to each other. However, this interpretation contradicted the next lines of the same text, according to which Eve was created after Adam and more specifically from his rib. Thus, she was inferior and posterior to him. How could these wise men cover up the blunder of their holy haste? How could Adam and Eve be equals in the beginning, but superior and inferior during the rest of the play?

A first wife was invented or recovered from the past, Lilith, and God was restored to magnanimity, as He made no discriminations between his first creatures. Full of goodwill, He created a man and a woman who were equal. But, woman being the incarnation of primordial evil, she could not be a heeding equal, she could not consent to being "less equal". So she fled paradise, never to come back. And in this way, God learned his lesson: Women do not deserve to be equal to men, even if men are willing to grant them equality. They simply cannot take equality. Did He ever think to make women superior to men? In no way! Women were to be inferior to men, so the creator created another woman, Eve, this time from Adam's rib.

Even this tale is inconclusive: If Eve was made from Adam's body, how was she different from him? It would be more rational to assume that that being the case, Eve should be the same as Lilith, the same as the man she was created from, the same as Adam. Or is it that the rib is a lesser part of the human body, therefore he (or she) who is born from it, is lesser too?

We saw that the tale of a first disobedient wife served as a cover-up for the inconsistency in the interpretation of the book of Genesis. The second use of the myth, is the moral teaching addressed to all women on earth. Do they really want to be considered equal to men? Do they think that they actually are men's' equal? They have another think coming. Let them see what happened to Lilith, the first trouble maker, ungrateful and disobedient to her husband and to her God, she fell from paradise, she became a demon. Women of the earth, beware, your place is in your kitchen and in your husband's bed.

Maybe the dogmatists of the time forgot that Lilith was not thrown out of the garden of God, she fled willingly. But at the time the scriptures were re-written for massive distribution, people lacked the education and the insight to see the difference, the fear and the hope of God was in everyone.

The love story of Adam and Lilith was rapidly forgotten. To the contrary, Adam and Eve remained as the primordial couple. According to the theoreticians of the church, Eve was created for recreational purposes, as life for Adam alone was too monotonous; too much perfection and no one to share it with. Hence Eve came as an afterthought, as an accessory in God's creation. Her role is purely decorative. In addition to the pejorative state she was born into, she also proved to be a liar and a cheat. She let Satan seduce her and in her turn she seduced her guileless, innocent man. It is she, the sinful, hairy-brained woman who is the source of all evil.

We came a long way, from Lilith the goddess of the first Jewish tradition to Lilith the demon, the evil night wind, and to Adam, the first ancestor. But we still have a long way to go, so let us not forget that those who wrote the Holy Scriptures, the Koran, the Vedic cosmology, the philosophies and the history of our world, are all men.

Let us put the gods aside for a while, in order to go back to their creatures / creators, the men and women, particularly the men, who because of the female conspiracy, still think that women are superior to them, as bearers of life.

However, because every dog has his day, one day the men of the tribe came back from a long-term hunt or from a reconnaissance expedition, only to find out that no new members had been added.

Only the pregnancies already started at the time of their departure had ended in childbirths. The repetition of this association "when we elsewhere, here no new children", revealed to men the terrible secret: Men too had their fair share in the continuation of the species.

And then, the "slaves" revolted. But as with every revolution instigated by derived creatures, who do not fully comprehend their role and their contribution in the action, brought in itself the seed of its own destruction.

We do not believe that those primary rebels knew that they were derived from women, because they lacked the appropriate technical equipment. But they were drunk with the wine of a double superiority over women: first, they were physically stronger from women, and second, they knew, or rather they thought they knew, that it was them who held the key to life. They also ignored the fact that sperm is abundant, while ova are a direct function of the number of women alive. The supporting roles actors were assuming leading characters. So, now was the time to dethrone the hateful enemy, who for centuries had been deceiving them by withholding the truth and who monopolized the mystery of the creation of life. They took great pains to erase every trace that would make known to those who would come later, that for ages their ignorance had given women the upper hand.

It is difficult to imagine that in matriarchal societies, women mistreated men. First of all women were not physically adept to cope in battle with men, and second, they had no reason to. Women gave birth to men (and to women) and raised them. Men, in return, protected women and their children. We could say that there was a natural distribution of work, and add that the relation between men and women were sort of contractual, there was a *quid pro quo*. However, all derived creatures are hateful and envious of the one they were derived from. This is how man hated woman and, given the opportunity, reduced her to a state of a hostel for fetuses or of an object of pleasure.

We might say that in a way, woman being by nature a child-bearer, things might have stopped there. Alas, man, intoxicated with his new found power, and being by nature what woman was not, that is aggressive, sometimes beyond control, developed some secondary characteristics, such as vengeance, ingratitude, and leadership aspirations not only over woman, but over every other element of the universe, other males included, hence his unmanageable competitiveness.

Led by his instincts and taking advantage of his superior physical strength, man reduced to zero the substance and the human dignity of woman. Having turned her into a pregnancy machine or an object of desire, he also developed polygamous tendencies, as pregnancy is usually the consequence of pleasure but, more often than not, the reason for exclusion from pleasurable activities, as pregnancy and pleasure do not usually go well together.

It would be a serious omission to leave out of this chapter the fact that certain primitive tribes considered women as their primary stock, suitable for the barter economy of the time, as they boosted the tribe, with a little help from men. But the chaotic obstetrics of nature, the rhythmic incessant pregnancies, the poor quality of food, made them succumb quickly. Thus they were rare, consequently valuable. Men took great pains to preserve their women in good condition so that they would trade them for other goods of primary necessity.

Things move on and man develops reason and becomes a reasonable being. His superiority and his sovereignty over the other creatures of the earth is confirmed and well established. He conceives the notion of family because he wants to make sure that he does not have to feed the offspring of another man's seed, either out of misunderstanding or out of deceit. In his endeavor he asks for and receives aplenty the help of organized religion. Family is hence sacred. Woman belongs to her husband and master, like an inanimate object, until he decides to throw her out and acquire a new model. It seems that the same notion of the woman-furniture has prevailed through the millennia, as in the film "In the year 2525", where women were referred to as furniture who went with the apartment.

She has no say in family or public affaires. He may treat her as he pleases. Romans used to call women "*sexus imbecilis*". As for the ancient Hellenes, particularly the democratic Athenians, they deprive her of all education because staying at home and bearing children does not require any. Only courtesans are exempted from this rule of ignorance and obscurity. The courtesan's task is to please men, but men, especially the educated ones, do not achieve ecstasy only by sex. Mere brutal sex was for the ignorant, the slaves and the servants; wives or simple prostitutes would suffice for these primitive needs. For the pleasure of the more sophisticated classes, courtesans have access to information on the political situation of the city, are aware of diplomatic incidents, take instruction on poetry, literature and philosophy. They are trained to be witty, and at the same time submissive. It goes without saying that they had to be pretty and that they were very studiously trained in the secrets of satisfactory lovemaking. We may safely guess that the Japanese geisha is an evolution of the ancient courtesan, who later developed into the Call girl of the western civilizations.

The irony lies in the fact that in democratic Athens, women were legally considered as second-rate citizens. In oligarchic Sparta, on the other hand, women were considered as equal, or rather less unequal, to men, and little girls sat side by side with little boys, in schools and in the barracks. Of course, even in Sparta, women did not accede to high officialdom neither did they go into the Spartan army. But their situation was not as lamentable as that of the other women of their times. Their education infused them with sentiments of patriotism and when their sons were leaving to go to the war, the mother would hand him his shield and tell him that he should either bring the shield back, or he should be brought back lying on it, having died an honorable death for his city.

Married women were excluded from the Olympic Games. Admission in the stadium was prohibited to them, as spectators of course, because the image of a woman athlete was at the time inconceivable. So mothers, sisters and wives of the participants, could not share this athletic event that imposed the truce on all armed conflicts on the Hellenic territory. To sum it up, all Hellenic male citizens, plus barbarians, slaves, virgins and the priestess of goddess Dimitra[3] had the lawful right to watch the games. It would be useless to analyze further the permission to the virgins. It was a not so subtle way to cultivate acquaintances among the young men and women.

---

[3] Dimitra was sister to Jupiter, and goddess of agriculture. She was also the mother of Persephone, who abducted by Pluto, king of Hades, spent six months with her husband in the nether world, and her mother's sadness at the separation made autumn and winter. Her uncle Jupiter, saddened by her mother's grief, arranged it so that the remaining six months (spring and summer) she would spend with Dimitra who was so happy that things bloomed and people harvested the fruit of the earth again.

For the sake of history, we will remind the reader of Kalipateira from the island of Rhodes, daughter of Diagoras, a renowned Rhodian champion of the Olympic games, mother of Peisirothos, also Olympic champion, and sister to other known athletes. On the morning of July 11th, 396 B.C., during the 96th Olympics, with her husband and coach of their son dead, she managed to slip in the stadium dressed as coach. But when she saw her son win, she jumped over the seats to join him at the podium. It was then that her clothes fell from her body and her sex was revealed. The judges and the rest of the dignitaries did not punish her, because her father exercised a considerable influence. However, in order to avoid being duped again, they ruled that hence, not only athletes, but coaches as well would enter the stadium naked.

Man does not show much affection for members of his own sex either. In his mind, he conceives majestic monuments that will glorify his name in the present and render his memory immortal in the future, but which he cannot build with his own two hands. So he uses the institution of slavery, induced mainly by captivity[4]. There is a Greek verb that unfortunately has not been translated in Latin (εξανδραποδίζω), which means to enslave and its etymological meaning is "to take the male – in the sense of human – element out of man, to reduce him to the state of non human". Man deprives his slaves of all means of self-defense; he obliges them to do heavy work, like building pyramids, temples, statues, roads, aqua ducts, baths, gardens, whole cities. In Rome, when no convicts from death row were available, they forced slaves to wrestle to death among themselves or threw them to the hungry beasts, for the pleasure of the crowds. Our well-admired gladiators came from the class

---

[4] According to Roman law, the child followed the social status of the mother, according to most barbaric laws it followed the social status of the father, while canon law, in order to erase slavery, stipulated that if any of the two parents was free, then the child would be free. Paupers were also known to sell themselves as slaves in order to find food, while insolvent debtors were sold to their creditors.

of the slaves. Slavery was officially abolished from the so-called civilized world in 1926[5].

The women of the defeated and sacked cities who were reduced to servitude, were burdened with tasks more compatible with their nature. The young and the beautiful, if they were lucky, were sent to the harems. There they had to cope sexually with one man, and they were kept in pleasant living conditions. The unlucky ones were sold to whore houses, where they suffered all abuse one can imagine. The ugly women slaves were either given domestic work, or were sent to work to death alongside men. The older ones were given domestic work or were trusted with the care of the children. However, almost none of them escaped the mass rapes that followed the defeat of their tribe. Individual rape or gang rape was mostly used, not only as a reward for the braves and as a release from the strain of the battle, but also as a means of psychological pressure to better achieve subjugation. It also helped sow the vanquished with the seed of the victors, ensuring in this way the rupture of the cohesion of their tribe and maybe the sprouting of a friendly nucleus in enemy territory. If we add that most of these women witnessed the slaughter of their men-folk, the burning down of their homes and all the atrocities that usually befell those who lose the war we can form an idea of the trauma that marked them for life.

These ordeals had extreme effects on slaves, men and women alike: either they broke down completely and were turned into submissive and obedient servants, or their will to flee slavery was steeled, and the rest of their life was consumed with this longing (and planning) for freedom. Sometimes, the passion for freedom cost them their life. When The Hellenes lifted the banner of liberation in order to rid themselves of the

---

[5] Convention of September 15, 1926. However, many Constitutions as early as the 19th century, dispose that "no man can sell himself", as men sometimes would sell themselves to rich masters, in order to survive in cases of extreme poverty.

ottoman occupation[6], declared that "it was better to live for only an hour, but free, than a life of forty years in slavery and in prison".

\* \* \*

"This reminds me", thinks Masculina to herself, "of what I must have read in another book, but I did not have the chance to verify it, that the only human race that did not practice slavery was that of the native Americans, which became extinct by the white man soon after he arrived there. It is easy to assume that if this were the case, before every battle the Chief would issue the horrible order: 'no prisoners'. Was it right? Actually, was it better to survive a battle just to end up a defeated slave, which in itself was a second chance, or was it better to die a free man? Is it fair that life – and dignity – could be determined by a blow of the tomahawk?" It is true that she has some difficulty in thinking of "man" as the representative of the human race; her upbringing intervenes arbitrarily and corrects her, substituting citizen for man. Slavery as well, is an institution entirely alien to her and to her race. But she keeps reading, at the end of the book she has her own conclusions to draw.

\* \* \*

Last but not least among the evils bestowed upon mankind by the rule of man, comes the tradition of torture. It is a safe guess that this - ancient as man - system applied to for the extraction of revelations, confessions and secrets, but also used as a means of punishment[7] during the middle ages in Europe and elsewhere, has been used under all regimes of male

---

[6] Turk occupation started on May 29th, 1453 with the fall of Constantinople, and ended, typically, on March 25, 1821, when the war against the enemy was declared. Actually, it took many decades, and the intervention of many European countries, for the whole of the Hellenic territory to be restored to the Hellenic authorities.

[7] ROUMAJON Yves (Dr.) *"Enfants perdus, enfants punis"*, ROBERT LAFFONT, Paris, 1990, p. 44 and following.

rule. Torture started as a custom when law was still oral, and later it was included in many written barbaric legal systems. It took more than ten centuries of Christian admonitions - and the Spanish Inquisition - to banish torture from the means available for the enforcement of law and order, as unacceptable and unpleasing to god.

Almost always torturers and executioners are men. Women have not the physical strength required, nor the sentimental stamina to put another living creature to unnecessary pain. Also let us keep in mind that, until the late 20th century and in order to keep the human race going, women could not escape from the pains of childbirth. Male torturers have studied the mysteries of pain and terror on living, human subjects (no guinea-pigs here), and most of them get a thrill out of it. They always know in advance that in the end, they will finish off their victim. They also promise a quick and clean death, if the victim complies with their wishes, in other words if the victim renounces his / her own religion, tells on his / her accomplices or if they simply repent. It is not the pure use of force that gives torturers their kicks. It is the fact that their victims are not free to defend themselves – if they can – but bound to the rack, or chained to the wall, that makes all the difference.

Mercifully, technology has been put to the service of those who have made their business to find out about other people's secrets: several chemicals may be used in order to confuse the victim and tear away every vestige of caution, reaching to the core of the subconscious and thus extracting all sorts of secrets. No sadistic interventions are needed any more. All it takes is a nurse to give the injection. The rest is the job of the trained psychologist. Soon, thought – and hoped – the scientists, the term "torturer" will be obsolete, and sadists will be once again called sadists.

However, this was not the case. The developments in the war in Iraq showed the world that chemicals or not, nothing is as good as the old traditional "methods of interrogation", as they have been euphemistically called by the American administration. What the civilized soldiers did to the uncivilized Muslim prisoners of war, the humiliation and the indignity of the methods used, makes one wonder what is the definition of civilization, and which nations can put a claim to it. This war also marked the willing participation of women not as victims but as interrogators. Another blow was delivered to the "civilized" world. Men were shocked to see female torturers being as effective as their male colleagues, women were surprised to see men being brutalized by women, and the general conclusion was that, if correctly trained, women can be very thorough interrogators. It seems that living in a man's violent world has seriously affected women and infected them with sadism and a tendency to violence.

Women have been known to be vengeful and sometimes sadistic, particularly when scorned by the man they (think they) love. But their motives have been strictly personal. Avenging themselves has sustained them when rejected. How contradictory, punishing someone whom you love because he does not love you. Also jealous lovers and husbands have been inflicting pain to the woman they love because she is suspected of having been unfaithful. The things people do for love!

Long as this list seems, we cannot forget that for a very long time, man considered even his own children as pests. In Europe until the 19th century, and in Asia and elsewhere until today, poverty has made parents, father and mother alike, to sell their children, either as apprentices to technicians, as slaves or, more often, to whore houses. The sale works both ways: in the first place, the child will learn an art that will assure its daily bread, and second, the family will benefit from the product of the sale. Sometimes, the children are rented. In this case, the family relies on the income this rent provides.

In the earlier days, wild sons and amorous daughters who compromised their family's good name and honor and its financial standing could well be sent away with the help of the state or the church, depending on the child's sex. A wealthy family could send the prodigal son to a forced labour colony, where the boy would be corrected by hard, read inhuman, work, while girls were sent away to convents, to become brides of the Lord and rid themselves of the sins of the flesh.

In misery stricken Hellas, during the ottoman occupation and for many years after liberation, parents had no other choice but to sell the children that god sent them, but which they were unable to raise themselves. The tale of the dance of the "one-legged, one-armed and blind man" as narrated by Karkavitsas[8] is heart renting: The leader of a gang of beggars comes to an agreement with a poor man, and every child the latter's wife bears, he hands to the dexterous hands of the former, who either blinds, or deafens or in any other ways makes the child handicapped. Then the crippled new born is presented to the mother, who, burdened with another invalid, cannot but give her ascent to rent the deformed child to the arch-beggar. Such a child is a great asset for his gang because it fills the well-to-do with sympathy and the bandit's pockets with the alms of this sympathy. It would be useful to add that the beggar's gang consisted of children who had either been born deficient, or had been purposefully deformed, in order to elicit pity from the healthy and wealthy. The purpose of the dance was to exercise the gang's members to show off as convincingly and as pitifully as possible their ailment. Finally the poor mother found out that all her babies had been born healthy but it was their father's treason that maimed them. What could she do, but kill herself.

Quite in the opposite direction moves the "murderess" of Alexandros Papadiamantis[9]. The author tells of a very poor couple that cannot afford to live on their own, so they stay with the wife's mother. In this way their misery is shared in three and not in two. There comes a time when the

[8] KARKAVITSAS Andreas, *'O Zitianos'* *(The Beggar.)* Estia, 1931.
[9] PAPADIAMANTIS Alexandros, *'I Fonissa'* *(The Murderess.)* Doric Publications, 1977.

young bride becomes pregnant and gives birth to a baby girl. The older woman is alarmed. How to raise a girl in such poverty, nobody will ask her to marriage, she will end up badly. Life goes on and the young woman bears another baby girl. Overwhelmed with despair, the grandmother takes both girls to a near-by well where she drowns them, in order to spare them the misery that is in store for them. Their parents are frantic about the fate of their missing girls and they go to the police. Soon all indications are against the grandmother. She cannot live anymore with the guilt for her crime and she also refuses to be judged by humans. Besides, she is well aware of her impending imprisonment and final and ungraceful death if they catch her. So she steps into the sea, where she vanishes under the waves. However, her crime and her sacrifice did not prevent little girls from being born and from suffering, ever after.

# MALE HOMOSEXUALITY

The ultimate indignity for woman comes when man deprives her from one of her two capacities, that of an object of desire, leaving her only child bearing to console her of her utility in this life. For many years, many civilizations, without praising openly homosexuality, considered it a natural phenomenon, caused by living together for years during military expeditions and far away explorations. Ancient Hellenes found a more profound and at the same time more subtle explanation. According to them, women were not cerebral enough for refined men. Plain women were for procreation only. Men who seek pleasure in women are lesser creatures like the receptacles they find pleasure in. Therefore, only brutal and ignorant slaves who liked women were tolerated. And those who wished to leave descendants.

But the woman is not man's sole target. Man is competitive, he wants to be master of the universe. He minimizes the woman's participation in decent life, he enslaves as many males as he can, but still, too many men are free, having the same aspiration as he: each and every one of them wants to be master of the universe. So man initiates other men in the secrets – and maybe pleasures – of homosexuality. Reducing one man to the state of a woman, means one competitor less. More homosexuals mean lesser men. Lesser and rare and more exotic. More dear. It is easier to subdue women and effeminate men than real men who all carry the same vain ambition: to contend for leadership.

However, this is only the rationalization of the phenomenon. The real cause is nature itself. When the male gene is by nature half female, it is male nature that betrays men. So nature betrays man, and man betrays man with homosexuality.

Male homosexuals are known to have existed since the dawn of time. In the Old Testament, the city of Sodom was punished by god because its citizens engaged in unhealthy (and non reproductive) pleasures. Usually the relation between master and apprentice cultivated the necessary mentality that ended up erotically. In this way, many old philosophers, who, as young men had had their fair share of womanizing, but who at their old age could not hope for nothing more than a prostitute's bought caresses, achieved a lively sexual life with young men, who, in their turn, let themselves be charmed by the mysteries of wisdom, religion, art, poetry, science and what not, in order to gain the favor of the master. Biographers of great men do not fail, every now and then, to amaze the public with stories of male lovers dug out from the past.

Common men, men of the arts but royalty as well formed such liaisons. Kings were particularly deluded when they had to marry for a *"raison d'Etat"*. Many historians are of the opinion that male homosexuality has been practiced not only among the noble, but also among the middle classes. Yet, it seems that male love was a luxury for those who could afford it. The poor had not the mental resources, nor the peace of mind that would permit them to try to convert other men to homosexuality. Besides, they needed children who, in the future, might work for them and lighten their misery. Male love has been observed not only in Europe, where a high degree of civilization permitted the indulgence in all sorts of love, but in other parts of the world as well. Particularly in tribes of traditional warriors, no amount of savagery shown to the enemy during battle could wipe out completely the sentiment of loneliness and the need for camaraderie that made two men turn in love to each other.

Play-acting was also the theater where men let their female substance take a free hand. Neither in ancient Hellas, nor in China until recently, were women permitted to become actors. Men enacted female characters.

Effeminate men. In *"Adieu ma concubine"*[10], the author describes very persuasively a young man's journey from male to effeminate to homosexual, through this play-acting training. Were women incapable of impersonating female roles? If we take into consideration that the meaning of the ancient Hellenic word for actor is ηθοποιός, which means "he who creates morals" and if we keep in mind that woman was considered as dirty, lowly and stupid, the answer to the question above could be yes. This does not exclude the fact that play-acting gave a free reign over the female side of men. On the stage, the actor impersonated a woman, he was not a woman, he was not a homosexual either. He was just a good actor.

But the times are changing. Relations between men do not produce children who will become warriors for the faith of our Lord, and consumers for the development of trade, and followers of their masters and fans of innumerable leaders. These men are not only useless; they are a danger to the Christian society and to all theocratic and totalitarian regimes that need soldiers as cannon fodder. Let them burn at the stake, let the eternal fires of hell consume their sinful bodies.

Literally they put them to the stake, together with the witches and those possessed by devil. During the dark ages, the fate of the homosexuals becomes worse than the fate of women. Even in recent years, Hitler did not hesitate to send them to the crematoria, together with the Jews, the gypsies and the politically undesirable. His supreme race could not tolerate the existence of men who would not reproduce this excellent specimen, the Aryan man.

Generally speaking, a person is either a man or a woman; there is no third way. Or is there?

---

[10] LEE, Lilian, *Adieu ma Concubine*, J'ai lu Publications, 1993.

The truth is that there is also another kind of men: those who are definitely not homosexuals, but who demonstrate the sensitivities of women. Woe upon them, as for ages sensitivity has been considered either an indication of latent homosexuality, or a prelude to it. Quite a lot of fathers of boys have spent sleepless nights, fretting that their son is not as manly as he should be. More often than not, sensitivity is a matter of youth. As the years go by and boys become men, the sensitivity of their early days gives its place to cynicism. But the fathers are not aware of this, and besides they cannot wait to see what will become of the manhood of their sons, because it may be too late by then.

So they hasten to take action, to put things in the right path, to make sure that no deviation from normal will occur. Needless to say that sometimes it is this worry that makes young boys turn to men for comfort. No sir, no son of mine will be a queer, a fag, a whatever. The first preventive measure taken is hunting. They take the boy hunting, and they force its active participation in killing. Or, if hunting season is still away, they order the boy to kill an animal. Usually it is an animal they love, a harmless animal, because they do not wish to put their son's life in danger by choosing a savage and dangerous beast. Should the boy be revolted by the sight of blood and by the inhuman task laid out for him, the unfortunate father believes that his wife gave him a gay boy for a son. Approximately at the age of sixteen, the second weapon comes forth: it is the obligatory visit to the downtown brothel, where the father is a regular customer. Many a tender boy's heart was crushed when forced to embrace the cynical and savage and life-ravaged prostitutes.

More reason and less fear made things easier for the sons of the African tribes. There, the boy has to learn the secrets of hunting in order to survive. So at puberty, the boy joins his elders at the hunt, and tries to become the best, thus winning respect, and an eligible bride. It is quite a different cultural and economical context that helps males remain male. In a more or less autocratic society, man has to bring his own food at the table; he cannot afford to adopt a different way of life. And if he does, the tribe will ostracize him, which is another risk he cannot afford; for these people, loneliness is not a viable option, it means isolation and eventually death.

Another factor that contributed to the inclination of a boy's mind towards homosexuality was a sort of punishment, used by tutors and teachers in boys' colleges in northern Europe. When a young student was caught doing something wrong, or suspected of having done something wrong (let us not forget that for centuries suspicion and indication – what we would call today "circumstantial or collateral evidence" – sufficed to condemn someone, no proof was needed) he had to drop his trousers and undergarments, present his posterior to the teacher or warden or principal and be beaten by rod or cane. How wisely was masochism cultivated, how easily feelings of guilt and of uselessness bloomed! How unwisely young men learned to expose a much sensitive area of their body, and leave it to the mercy of another man!

Last but not least, come the boys who have had been raised by their mother, while the father is either dead, or missing, or has left them for another woman. The son must take the place of his father and remain faithful to the mother, and not start dating with girls. The poor mother deserves this loyalty from the son, which the father did not offer. Hasn't she sacrificed her life and her own sexuality in order to raise him by keeping aspiring step-fathers at bay? Hasn't she always been alone without a mate? It is the son's obligation to do the same, to take care of her and to spare her of the antagonism a young bride would bring into her household. Some mothers praise openly the sons of other women who have always been at their mother's beck and call. These mothers push their sons, indirectly but all too clearly towards homosexuality. They do not care if their son will be happy or not, all they care about is their own well-being.

In this case it is the mother who undermines maleness, and she does it indirectly and insidiously. Its very foundations are creaking, ready to fall apart. The woman-mother subtly and sentimentally blackmails the young man-son to moderate his preferences to suit her own needs and appetites.

As the young man grows up he gradually discovers that he is different from other men. Usually after some internal fight he accepts his homosexuality and is ready to live with it. But he also finds out – usually the hard way – that others are not. The father is always contemptuous of his gay son, the mother is more tolerant, his comrades at school attack him verbally and physically, women sympathize with him. He learns to dissimulate the fact that he is homosexual, and, in the older days, when homosexuality was a crime, he used to be quite successful.

But what about female homosexuality? Are women absolutely straight? Certainly not! However, until the early 21st century, homosexual men were more that their female counterparts. Female nature is homogenous (XX), so, genetic anomalies apart, it is usually after an incestuous rape or, even worse, continuous incestuous rape that woman turns to another woman for sexual relief. Women can also be bisexual without any noticeable change in their feelings or in their behavior. Women always feel the void in their body that must be filled. Whether they will choose a man to do it for them or another fellow woman, it is simply a matter of trust. But their nature remained unchanged, whereas the man who tends to homosexuality has changed his nature, he finds pleasure in being a woman.

There is also a small portion of the female population that is sentimentally lazy; they are reluctant to exert themselves in order to build a fulfilling relationship with a member of the other sex, so they find refuge in women, which – they think – is easier. Human relations are never easy, be it with members of the same or of the other sex.

It can easily be presumed that women rarely seek pleasure in women – just like some men. Behind the name that is used to describe them, a whole history lies forgotten; long wars had deprived the women of the Hellenic island of Lesbos of their men, so they could not find relief but among themselves. It was necessity that drove them, not preference or choice.

This 21st century changed things radically. Homosexuality is no more the privilege of men. Women are no more forced by circumstances to opt for women. They chose freely, openly and quite provocatively to spend their life with members of their own sex. The questions that arise are numerous: were women always crypto-homosexuals very adept in dissimulation, or was it a sort of retaliation to the ever expanding male homosexuality? Were they fed up with men who had to be either macho or gay? Was this phenomenon the natural development of a gay society?

What about the Amazons? Does this mythic society fall into the same category as homosexual women? Tradition has it that its members were women warriors who used to cut off one of their breasts, so that they would use the bow and the arrows unhindered. However, they were not lesbians. Quite the contrary, they welcomed men among them. But they had a bad habit; when men had outlived their purpose and utility which was a simple carnal relation with the utter purpose of potential impregnation, they killed them as useless or dangerous to the matriarchal structure of their society. What happened to the baby boys that were born? Could it be that the Amazons were wise enough to have found a way to conceive only girls? Because it is difficult to imagine that apart from the fathers, they also killed their baby-boys at birth. Or, even worse, that they let them live until they were ripe for mating and then disposed of. In this case, internal breeding would have caused the degeneration of the tribe. Or did it actually happen like this?

# WOMAN, A SECOND RATE CITIZEN
## Year 125.897, Safeland

Language is the expression of a civilization. It is no accident that in most European languages "man" has a double meaning: the human and the male. For example, we say that "man – or l'homme, l'uomo – has reason, while animals do not". On the contrary, the Hellenic language, ancient and modern, always has had and still has two different words for these two different notions: ἄνθρωπος for human, and ἄνδρας for male. Ἄνθρωπος has no sex; he can be either man or woman. But for most Europeans it goes without saying that male and human are one and the same. *A contrario*, woman is not human. To our knowledge, the only other linguistic exception is the German language, the grammar and the syntax of which are largely based upon the ancient Hellenic language.

Here is a question: What is the meaning of the Hellenic word "misanthrope" - which still perseveres in most languages of Greek origin - "he who hates people" in general or "he who hates males"? The answer can be easily provided: given the fact that the respective word for females is "misogynist" with a meaning which is crystal clear: "he who hates women", we may safely assume that misanthrope means he who hates males. However, this is a false assumption; a misanthrope is a loner, someone who does not want any people around, he hates even the sight of other humans. In the remotest possibility that a person might hate only males, no one took the trouble to invent a suitable word for such feelings.

The linguistic scorn apart, let us see how the living conditions of women developed through time.

The barbarian northern tribes that overwhelmed Europe after the fall of the Roman empire, brought with them their own laws. One of them is the salien law, according to which, women have no claims on the ancestral land. Traditionally, all land belonged to the king, who distributed it to his braves, in exchange for their services in war and their active support in peace time. When the beneficiary died, his estate went only to his male offspring, as daughters could not bare arms for the wars or the defense of their king, which was the only legal excuse for the possession of the land.

Initially, the law that concerned only the land-fief was extended to the throne-kingdom. The only legitimate heir to the throne was the male heir. But things change, as the husbands of the daughters laid claim on these fiefs and on these thrones. However, until the 19th century most European constitutions excluded expressly women from the throne. One of the few exceptions to this rule is the United Kingdom, where some of its queens have written glorious pages in the history of the country.

Except for the case of England, in most parts of the world the queen is the wife of the king, and her task is to give him heirs, male preferably. In the end, the feminist movement brought with the 20th century, erased this rule from the civilized legislations. But it is still valid in most Muslim countries where women have no rights whatsoever.

Speaking of Muslim women, it is the turtle that comes to mind; as the turtle carries its home on its back, in the same way the Muslim woman walks about clad in her fortress, her *bourca*. You cannot tell one woman from the other, not by her figure, nor by her hair, nor by her smile, because she has no reason to smile too often. Only a glimpse of her eyes, usually cast to the ground, may be permitted to the passer-by. You might be able to distinguish her by her voice, but then again, she is not permitted to say much, especially she can never say "no" to her husband

and master. Nobody knows if she is still alive, and nobody really cares; it is so easy to make a Muslim woman disappear from the face of the earth.

We remain in the sphere of the Koran, but we turn to the south, to Africa. There, a mixture of Christian Puritanism and misogynous Muslim beliefs, have led to the practice of the "surgical" removal of the clitoris with the simultaneous stitching of vaginal lips of young girls. Which pain to assuage first? What hurt to caress and what wound to staunch? How to explain to the victim the necessity of this atrocity? No clitoris guarantees no sexual arousal, consequently that the merchandise has not been spoiled, while the stitching is the seal against all intruder, sexual arousal or not. And what happens with the lawful husband during the first night? No surgical operation is available, his masculinity will have to literally tear down all obstacles. The pain of these women has no end; it seems that they are punished for being female.

\* \* \*

"Thinking about virginity makes me wonder if nature is actually a man or if the Christian God really exists and created the world to suit exactly the needs of his chosen creature, man. Because, what is the use of the virginal hymen if not to assure the male that his female and the offspring that will come later, belongs exclusively to him? Only the human female has been burdened with this anomaly, no other inhabitant of the earth has ever known such restrictions to its pleasure and to its breeding. Only the human male has been so inconsiderate as to establish such inhuman customs. Of course, I know what the authors of this history book did not at the time, as it happened millennia later: that this obstructive hymen gradually disappeared, as the period where girls entered active sexual life quite early gave way to asexual females and love-making subsequently vanished from the list of human activities." Masculina tries to suppress the fury that rises in her every time she encounters human (or natural) follies. She wants to go on with her study. However, the dormant male in her can neither suppress a frisson of pleasure as she imagines herself as the male conqueror who deflowers the virgin princess of the defeated fortress. Her initial resistance, so futile, the urgent and unrelenting pressure from his part, the final brake-in, her blood, her agony and her pain, her broken pride and her broken hymen to a man she hates and who maybe in the future will learn to love and to serve willingly. So stimulating!

\* \* \*

In some African Muslim countries where the *sharia* still applies, women who commit adultery, willingly or unwillingly (the latter is the case of rape), are lapidated to death. In the case of *Amina Lawal* in the year 2003 modern technology helped save her life, as activists for the women's rights all over the world protested through the Internet against the death sentence by lapidating, imposed on her on the grounds of adultery. However, no punishment has been provided for the man who commits adultery. It is amazing that in these countries, the Koran law is still valid only against the (inappropriate) behaviour of the women: Penalties that have been considered as barbaric regarding male offenders have been abolished: for example cutting the nose of the thief at first offence, his thieving hand in case of recurrence, has been given up since the late 20th century. He can enter a university, play foot-ball, find himself as many mistresses as he can afford to, while she will stay locked up at home, and should another male come along and "spoil" her, she will pay the price with her life. Useless to say that if *Amina* was spared this terrible death, the tribunals of her country continued to put women to death by lapidating for adultery. What a wonderful world!

But Africa and the Muslim world are so far away – are they really? The treatment of women there is an extreme and exceptional case. So if this is the exception, what is the rule?

The European women, daughters and wives of barbarians who aspired to revive the roman system, some of them even the ancient Hellenic regime, but always within the limits of their own traditions and customs, have lived an oppressed life. Mercifully they were luckier than their sisters of Africa and Asia as the cult taught by Jesus Christ and his apostles preached love for the fellow human. Christian religion considered women – not exactly on the same level as man, man is always the master – less human than man, but human all the same. Women have always been subject to men, regardless of their social status.

The ladies of the higher social classes, having delegated all duties of nurturing, housekeeping and sexual male satisfaction to the servants, were free to live a life of pleasure and leisure. But they had to be beautiful, according to the aesthetic standards of their time, always set by men. So they crushed their flesh in corsets and stays. Many a young girl felt her breath taken away the moment the maid tightened the strings of their corset. But this is not such a high price to pay for the sustenance they assured from their husbands or fathers.

They also had to be witty but not too clever, and they had to keep the residence of the master free of the turmoil of the babies. So the newborns were trusted to wet nurses, who were usually sent to their villages, with their own babies and madam's new baby, usually with a meagre monthly allowance. If the newborn managed to survive the filth and the indifference of the nurse, who, as often as not had no husband but many babies of her own, it was a matter of pure chance. Besides, if a baby died, who really cared, God would send another one along. This custom is one of the factors that contributed to the soaring of post-natal infantile mortality sky-high.

Of course, the nurse was not supposed to teach the child manners. So, when, at the age of four or five and having successfully surmounted the jealousy and the meanness of the other children of the household, the child was driven back to its parents' premises, a special instructor had to be hired, to help insert the child in its rightful environment. What a cultural shock; from the nurse's pig-stay to the family mansion, from the foul- mouthed and unwashed children that constituted his play-mates to the well spoken siblings and cousins, from the poorly cooked food to the exquisite delicacies and the lavish meals that their parents' table provided!

Today no family, no matter how rich, thinks of giving the babies away. Since the early 20th century, rich households can afford to place their care in hired hands, but always in the same residence as the rest of the family and under the supervision of the parents. This phenomenon was extinct because mentalities have changed, children are not considered any more as dangerous and annoying, just a step away from the ignorant beast, but as creatures of God since sometime before their birth, who deserve all the legal protection they can get. This practice disappeared together with the economic extreme gaps. Besides, the miracles of technology have considerably facilitated the care of the baby.

The women of the lower classes were less fortunate. The middle classes would train their daughters to become teachers – the term was "governess" – a dignified and relatively safe profession. Their merchant fathers were obliged to give them a dowry or else no man would marry them. If they could get themselves a husband, their existence was, more or less, secured. They had access to better medication and better nutrition, always within the limits of the scientific knowledge of their era. But all in all, they were in a better condition compared to their proletarian sisters.

The most expendable human beings were the women of the poor. Less restricted by moral principles, because nobody cared to teach them and because nobody cared what the morals of the daughter of a beggar were. They enjoyed the pleasures of love and sin, and paid dearly for them. Their life was usually short due to lack of sanitation and proper medical care. Servants, nurses, cheap prostitutes and later workers in the factories, they bore children in and out of wedlock, but their lives were usually dismal and unhappy, their lonely end a blessed release from misery.

As their rich sisters, they too had to give their children away to nurses, but for a totally different reason: they had to work ungodly hours, from dawn to midnight, in order to survive. It stands to reason that their income was too uncertain and too insufficient to sustain the baby in the nurse's care. The baby's life was in direct proportion to the fee paid by the mother to the nurse. In some cases, even a regularly paid fee could not ensure the baby's well being, as nothing and nobody could stop the nurse from mistreating, selling or starving the baby to death.

As a matter of fact, European women fared better than women in other cultures. The Hellenic, the roman and the Christian element of the European culture saw to the eventual humanisation of the barbaric laws brought with the barbarian invaders. However, they have always been considered as second rate citizens, their opinion has never been asked for, they are regarded as charges that a man – because he is conscientious – willingly accepts to be burdened with.

The key to a citizen's status, apart from birth, is education; in the case of women, the key was how to withhold education from them. Even the most privileged among them, did not have to know much; a little reading and writing, some elementary arithmetic, poetry, some works of great authors, some French and maybe some German were more than sufficient for young daughters and wives. They were also considered utterly accomplished if they did a lot of needlework.

The father who permitted or, even worse, imposed, further education on his daughter, was laughed at not only by his peers, but by the whole town. "What does she need all this education for", they would gossip among themselves, "has the father's fortune perished in imprudent investments, or in philandering, or in betting and now he has to send his daughter to work as teacher?"

No matter what theologists, philosophers, naturalists and other scientists have said about the inferiority of women's humanness, she has always been a human being, with her meagre reason (because of lack of education) and her ambitions (which are totally compatible with human nature). So she has always wanted to be a part of everyday life, to have a say in the family affairs. But her father has always searched to pass her on to a husband, and the husband, once found, at best ignores her and forbids her to speak her mind, or at worst mistreats her. How can she become a factor in the development of her family's life? It is quite simple: all she needs is a son; a fresh, virgin mind, a *tabula rasa* on which she will inscribe her own glory.

So the myth begins: she glorifies the fact that she is his mother, the carrier of her son's life, she stresses the sacrifices she has had to make so that he could grow up to be a happy and proud young man, the labour pains, the sloppy or unfaithful father whom she has tolerated in order to keep the family together. In other words she makes a monument out of motherhood and a martyr out of herself. She teaches him to respect her and to feel obliged for her sufferings. But she will not stop there. She implants in her son the scorn that all men feel towards women. Only she, the mother, is spared, because she accomplished her holy mission, to be his mother. This is how men who are called "their mother's son" are created. This is how numerous marriages and relations have been falling apart.

If we decide to take a closer look into the reasons for this behaviour, we shall see that women realised that they had no chance to influence situations. They were excluded from all levels of decision-making. The only way open to them was the oblique way: if they could not make the husband listen, they would make the son. And they wanted to keep this man to themselves they do not intend to share his respect with other women. "No one loves you like mama, my dear", they keep telling him every time they get a chance. The poor son, satisfactorily brain-washed, ends up believing that women are good or bad, but mama is the best.

The son who has been raised like this, turns into an obedient husband. His wife will take the place of his mother (after the death of the latter of course), if not in his heart, at least in his mind. Such households are run by the wife, as the neighbours whisper behind the husband's back.

And if the man, notwithstanding his poor mother's efforts to turn him into an obedient subject, becomes like his father, like all the other men of his generation, what does the wife do? She becomes the fragile doll, who cries so easily, who faints all the time, whose smelling salts must always be close at hand. As many men claim, the weak sex is not weak at all. It is true that the weaker rule the stronger by imposing their weakness, by presenting it as a cause of unmerited suffering, and by soliciting their protection.

But a reason other than the mother's exclusive possessiveness for her son may well lie in hiding behind her tactics: jealousy. The green-eyed monster will not allow mothers to make a better world for their daughters, by teaching their sons to respect all women. "What I have been through, scorn and violence and indifference, you will go through as well", they seem to say to their daughters. "Look for your vindication through your own son, not through mine, whom you will now take away from me by marriage. I didn't spend my entire life to make him respect me, even if no one else does, and then offer him to you, ready. No, you must fight your own wars."

Maybe this sounds too mean. Maybe we must look for yet another reason, which is insecurity, originating in ignorance. The women of that era, who had been raised to be only decorative or subsidiary elements, were not armed to survive alone, to make a stand. They did not have the knowledge that would help them claim their rights, neither the professional education that would lead them to their independence. They had to live within the confines of a male-ruled family. The time was not ripe yet for a change.

Besides, women of a certain social standing were not permitted to work. A working woman was a poor woman, a poor man's wife. A woman who went to work for an employer was anathema to her husband or father. A woman was sustained either as a daughter or as a wife. Naturally mothers would endanger their daughters' existence if they taught them things that were unacceptable to their keepers. In addition to the menace to the husband's economic reputation, sexual harassment, always imminent and always attributed to the woman's wantonness, was another threat to the husband's moral situation. These were the apparent pretexts for keeping their women knitting and stitching at home. Deeper fears were rooted in this isolation, which became known around the middle 20th, with the development of psychoanalysis: men were (rightly) afraid of the competition of women working alongside, of the unemployment that would befall the world, and of course of the economic independence that would make women indomitable. The whole edifice of the male-dominated world would come apart.

Finally, let us not forget another aspect of the economic factor: the inheritance of the fortune, when and where it existed. In Europe, whole estates were entailed away from the female line, which meant that at the death of the husband, his widow and his unmarried daughters were left at the mercy of the deceased's heir who could be a son, a brother or a distant cousin. It seems unlikely that women could do anything else but find themselves a husband. When their survival was at stake, who would look for love, respect, and other abstract nouns?

In royal families, the marriage of their children was simply a matter of securing an alliance between nations, while in the most affluent ones a firm merging or at least a means to avoid social decline because of a dwindling fortune. Love was redundant both in poverty and in riches.

Women of no education, reluctant to accept or even suspicious of all change – if it were again for the worse? – have contributed, with the help of their families, of the state and the church, to the preservation of this man ruled world.

Here is an example which is very often used in Political science courses: In a laboratory of physical science, female apes have been put in a cage, for observation. Later, a male ape is introduced into the cage. No breach of normal activity is observed. The next day the scientists reverse the experiment, confining male apes in the cage. As soon as the female ape is introduced, the males go crazy. They start to tear at each other, each wanting the female for his mate, until humans have to intervene in order to prevent a blood bath. It is easy for us to draw our conclusions, yet we would rather let the readers search for their own.

# MAN AND DEATH

The reasonable human being, man or woman, conscious of his or her insignificance and powerlessness in the universe, have always been seeking the sublime, the supernatural, the divine, that will help them, but who will also take all responsibility, as superior, for all human shortcomings. How convenient to be able to say "God willing, I will settle my debt to you".

The first gods were female, because of the primitive matriarchal societies. We thus have Artemis for the Hellenes or Diana for the Romans, goddess of virginity, of the moon, and of hunting. The moon has had a double significance for the first women: it could be a hunter's assistant or his death, so it had to be propitiated. It was also felt that it regulated women's menstrual circle and their fertility. Then Dimitra came, goddess of the earth, bringing to humanity the gift of agriculture, and the moon lost its preponderance, it had to cede its place to the sun, that was beneficial to all plants. Later Juno, spouse of Jupiter comes forth to protect matrimony and childbirth, Aphrodite or Venus, goddess of love and pleasure, and Hestia or Vestia, protector of the household. The goddess of wisdom came later, and she was given the name of Athena or Minerva.

The core of all female beliefs is life and all that protects and encourages it; the household, fertility, love, nutrition. All ancient civilizations have had their respective goddesses.

On the contrary, man, deprived of the life-giving force, has focused his faith on death; death fascinates him, and around death he builds his religion and his science. He is afraid of his own death but he is desirous of the death of the other.

Man made his gods in his own image. The cosmogony of the ancients, those who shattered the societies run by the females and established the new order, is full of human passions. Father Uranus imprisoned his children, the Titans, the Giants and other primeval forms of life in the abysses of Earth, his wife. Could it be that this imprisonment shows that he never let them be born? Did he already know the secrets of contraception, or probably he was an early abortionist. One way or the other, he did not want to lose his throne to the vindications of his heirs.

No matter how hard he tried to avoid this, mother Earth desperately wanted a son, to love her and respect her, so she probably tricked him into letting out one of their sons, Cronus or Saturn. The son then liberated his siblings, in order to overthrow their selfish father. Saturn and his brothers managed to send their daddy to the skies and make him a planet, while he kept his mother, Earth, to tread upon. He also threw his brothers back inside their mother's depths. He took his sister Rhea as wife, who gave him lots of sons and daughters. But he would not let happen to him what he did to his father, he would not trust his spouse. So he ordered his wife to bring him each newborn child for inspection, which then he devoured. In other words, he did not trust his wife with his sperm. Despite his precautions Rhea, daughter of her mother, frustrated and childless after so many births, when she was delivered of her last son, she took a stone, wrapped it up as a baby, and presented it to her husband. Saturn did not much care to see the face of his child, he just wanted to make sure that no one would ever come forward to dethrone him.

This incident can be attributed to the possibility that Rhea escaped from her husband's vigilance and substituted the contraceptive herbal concoction with a harmless one.

He was soon disillusioned when his son Zeus or Jupiter, after having been raised away from the sight of his father, in a cave in Crete under the care of a goat, Amalthea, returned, freed his uncles and siblings from bondage in the core of the earth – we do not wish to consider an oedipal complex with the grand-mother – and at this point, the powers were divided, though no woman took the blame for this; some sided with Cronus against his rebel son, some allied themselves with the latter. The Jupiter coalition soon got the upper hand, and Saturn had to surrender. No sooner was he obliged to vomit up the children he had devoured, and his son also castrated him, so that a definite end was put to his line. His genitals were thrown to the firmament, where, most probably became planets too.

Jupiter chose mount Olympus for the divine residence, took one of his sisters, Hera or Juno, as wife, and ruled gods and men alike. But his war allies became restless, they wanted part of the glory for themselves, they became a pest. War erupted between the gods on the one side, the titans and giants on the other. The gods won, their uncles and aunts were thrown back where they belonged. No one remained to contest the primacy of cloud-leading Jupiter.

After some time, a remarkable birth occurred in the kingdom of the gods: Athena, the goddess of wisdom, was born from the head of her father Jupiter. The myth says that for many days, the god had been suffering from an acute headache. One day his forehead broke open (historians claim that his brother Hephaestus, god of fire and smithery was summoned to lend his assistance to the supreme god with his hammer) and out stepped the goddess. It is no accident that the only male that ever managed to father and mother his child was a god. No mortal could achieve this much-envied faculty of womanhood. It is also no accident that the goddess of wisdom could not be born of a woman, by nature a stupid and inferior creature. The myth of Athena's birth gives a spiritual and cerebral – both incompatible with women – aspect to procreation and birth.

In this world created by man (male) for man, woman has no other place but that of life-bearer, like Earth and Rhea, in any way she can. Life in itself is excluded, as men, fathers, brothers, sons and uncles kill each other, in order to become the only source of power and to preserve their sovereignty.

Then Christian religion came along, and the position held by women was considerably upgraded. Although still inferior to man, she participates in the arrival of Christ – as an incubator, she is part of the holy family though not of the holy Trinity. This holy Trinity has been many a child's nightmare: it consists of a father, a son, and a spirit. Where is the wife of the former and mother of the latter?

As the young Christian grows up, he learns that although Mary does not belong to the holy Trinity, she is the intermediary between god and man. Christians always turn to the mother of Christ when matters of life, health and wayward children, arise. She seems to be the christianised version of the ancient goddesses, all six of them in one deity (it looks like the spirit of economy is as old as man).

Jesus taught that all people are equal in the eyes of God. What he truly meant is that men must not mistreat women, because they, too, have a soul. He raised them from the status of *res*, but not to that of man. She is always inferior to him. The apostles did not fail to exhort woman to obey her father first and then her husband, as superior to her.

During the mystery of marriage we hear the priest of the Orthodox Church chanting "woman must be in fear of man". Customarily, this is the time when the bride steps down hard on the groom's toe, to let him know that she will not be afraid of him. But the message of the holy fathers is clear: "Women, beware of your men. Do not love them, do not respect them, do not be companionable, just be afraid of them".

However, it is not to be thought that the relations between man and woman suffice to define the Christian dogma. Essentially it is a scenario of death lust, inconceivable at least for a woman. The father sends his son – does the son exist already or has he been specifically invented for this mission – among men, to die a horrible and undignified death in order to redeem humanity from the primordial sin which was the work of Eve. His blood will wash humanity of its filth; he will defeat death by death. To solidify this redemption, he offers his body to be eaten and his blood to be drunk so that he will be remembered. The sacrament of the Holy Communion is thus established in Christian practice. Eating one's god and drinking his blood is an extremely ancient custom characteristic to paganism. Its purpose was to convey to the eater the qualities of the perishing god. This custom had to be preserved in order to facilitate conversion from paganism to the Christian dogma. The new religion had to include some elements of the previous one, so that the people would not be shocked into a totally new theory. Since that time, Christians have thankfully been drinking the blood and eating the body of Christ!

Is it of any consequence the fact that God, after Abraham dutifully obeyed His command and offered up his son to be sacrificed, ordered his people to stop all sacrifices – particularly human sacrifices – in his name? Or that He ordered them, through Moses, to stop all sacrifices because it was a pagan custom? Did he reserve the ultimate sacrifice exclusively for his son? People usually try to defend their religion, and they come up with soul-stirring justifications. However, when questions become pressing, the answer is that God's will is sometimes incomprehensible to man, that He acts in mysterious ways.

Jesus promised mortals that those who lived by his teachings would gain the kingdom of heaven, the celestial kingdom. Most religions promise another life to their faithful, because man cannot be satisfied with his life, nor with his fate. He cannot accept that he may be simple stardust, dust motes carried hither and thither by the wind, his existence an infinitesimal quantity of time in all eternity. He craves for what he can never have, eternity. So he invents an eternal life after death, in heaven for himself and in hell for his enemies. In a way, this after-life consoles him for the insignificance of his present life and at the same time condemns those who are different from him to the eternal sorrows of hell.

The book of Genesis informs us that in heaven, in the ancient Garden of Eden, there was the tree of knowledge of good and evil. The fruit of the tree, knowledge, was forbidden to the first couple of creation, under the penalty of eviction. In this way man, the myth-maker, says indirectly that knowledge is not desirable, darkness and ignorance and blind faith to our lord is the only key to paradise. Man does not need to know, it suffices that god does. "Believe and ask not" becomes the motto. How artfully obscurantism passed for a divine directive!

Of course, some scholars do not agree with this thesis: "Search in the Scriptures" they advise. It is remarkable that they do not advocate knowledge in general, because for them, the only source of knowledge is the word of god. The matter is, how the word of god is interpreted. Law has always been subject to interpretation, and the law of god is no exception. So, he who searches in the Scriptures, will most probably find what he is looking for.

Man could not escape his nature, he had an almost perfect god, but he could not leave him untarnished from human passions. So the story of Cain and Abel, the first murder in biblical history is explained as a result of the primordial sin – evil is always a woman's fault. Also the story of Esau and Jacob shows how greed and plotting and deceit are inserted in the weave of human life – with the help of the mother who wanted to see her favourite son accede to a place that was lawfully the place of his brother. It is also a case of knowing good and evil and applying the latter.

The other most wide spread religion on our planet, is that of Mohamed. But is it truly a religion, or a perfectly simulated instrument of imperialist policy? The Islamic motto "Death to the infidels" sounds like a demagogic command that flourishes in the darkness of ignorance. Before the prophet arrived to enlighten the Arabian tribes, they excelled in astronomy, medicine and mathematics. When the prophet left them for the Muslim heaven, religious fanaticism erased all other preoccupation. To prove their obedience to their god's word, they expanded to the south covering the whole of Africa and from there to the west conquering Spain and even attempted to go north to France, where Charles Martel put a stop to their aspirations in the battle of Poitiers[11]. At the same time the Turks moved first to the east, proselytising – by force – vast areas of Asia, then to the west, where they conquered Constantinople and almost the whole of Hellas, to be finally stopped in Vienna.

However, it was the Arabs who saved the ancient Hellenic manuscripts from the destructive wrath of the Christian crusaders. The Christian knights wanted to wipe out everything that pertained to the old pagan civilization and the faithless Muslims prevented them, showing an admirable tolerance for the Greek philosophy, or so some historians claim.

The Christian kings of Europe managed to resist the Muslim expansionism. It was their faith and the Hellenic and Roman origins of their culture that would not permit the establishment of foreign ideas and *a fortiori* of foreign religions. No idea, be it political, religious or moral can take root in a soil other than the one where it originated. The case of religion in Latin America shows clearly that no matter how hard the Christian missionaries worked to proselytise natives to the true religion of our lord Jesus Christ, no matter how violent the methods applied and how the people were finally forced to accept Christianity as the official

---

[11] 732 A.D.

religion of all the countries, secretly they stuck to their old traditions. Most of them really believed in the new religion that, rigorous as it was against sin and pleasure, offered the solace of love as a remedy from everyday hardships and the promise of a better life in the kingdom of god. And yet, few of them truly renounced their old pagan convictions. Few of them did not seek help from voodoo magic when the Christian god would not or could not help. Apparently the official religion is the one imposed by the missionaries, but underneath, the clandestine cult of magic, the cult of their ancestors, thrives. The traditions handed down to us by our ancestors are sacred and must be honoured, because they are the roots of mankind in the past, and its link to infinity.

As with religion, the same can be said about political ideas. When Alexander the Great conquered vast territories in Asia, he brought to the conquered peoples the notions of democracy, of free disposition and all the Hellenic ideals. But neither the minds, nor the temperaments, nor the mentality of the people could truly accept and assimilate them. Maybe not even the climate, or the soil, were favourable to the innovative morals brought from far away.

Muslim paradise is considerably more human than the Christian. It promises the earthly pleasures of abundant food and an unending supply of the ever immaculate houris. It is a paradise invented by men for men. As a result, the young men are not entirely to blame if they prefer the after life to the one they are now living, as some of their nations are on the brink of political extinction. They defend their existence with the most effective method: suicidal missions stirred by religious fanaticism. Who said that religion is the opium of the people? It can very well be its wildest and most uncontrollable stimulant.

Paradise, Christian and Muslim alike, is the promised reward for the faithful and the obedient; a credit and debit transaction, where man gives his full support to his church, conforms his behaviour and his life to its teachings, and in return he will be rewarded with happiness; but in the next life, where he will not be able to control, to check accounts, to protest, to contest, to press charges, to ask for his money back should he feel cheated!

Death scares and at the same time fascinates man. Particularly man is attracted to the death of the other, the adversary, the different, to the death of the enemy. These contradictory feelings resulted in the development of a defensive medicine, which for ages has been limited to curing and treating, and very recently (and theoretically) to prevention. He finds euthanasia repulsive; he classifies it among the criminal acts. So he condemns the already condemned terminal patient, intubated and dependent, to an undignified, painful and slow death.

But murder, even in cold blood, does not shock him. To the contrary, there is always a good reason to kill someone who has been bothering you. Hence the theory of the criminal psychology that claims that "given the right circumstances, we are all potential killers". As a result, his law tends to protect the rights of those found guilty, it guarantees them a fair trial and a good lawyer who will find the proper "attenuating circumstances" which will see to the acquittal of his client, no matter what he has been accused of. In solidarity to the condemned – if we are all potential killers, we may all end up behind bars if we get caught – the capital punishment is abolished and the principle of the necessity of the penalties makes life easier for them.

Besides medicine, man has also developed technology, this time of an offensive nature. Technology can be miraculous if put to the service of man, and nightmarish if put to destructive ends. This duality evokes the image of a man walking hurriedly; in one hand he holds a bottle of penicillin, in the other the formula for the H-bomb. How many lives to save with the one, how many to destroy with the other! Why is he almost running? Why is he in a hurry to cure his fellow men? So that they will be healthy when they disintegrate into thin air when the bomb explodes?

In a utopic world, technology would be friendly to the environment and helpful to mankind. But man managed to reverse things, in our days technology is a synonym for pollution and slow but certain death of all life. Even our planet is now in danger, and its survival is at best dubious.

# THE MACHO MAN WAS HERE!

Action breeds reaction, so man, faced with the menace of his emasculating active mother, decides to put up his defences. Most often than not, macho man is the son of tough father who is a role model to the child, or the son of a mother who taught him to despise all the world, and women in particular as unworthy, petty and stupid creatures.

The macho man puts on his lion hide, and with the help of his cudgel imposes his will. His wife will not work outside the house, his forehead is unblemished and will remain so, he is always right and the others always wrong, and as infallible and just, he is always the first to cast the stone. He believes that when reason is not a sufficiently persuasive method, a good beating never fails. Some of them do not even take the time to reason, they proceed straight to the beating, or to persuasion through the cudgel.

Women are not his only victims. Man or woman will fall under his cudgel, on one condition; that they are weaker. In his mind, it is him against the rest of humanity. Brutal force is not his only weapon; he has principles, preferably the traditional ones, and he makes it his business to see that they are strictly applied by the others. There is only one exception; his superiors. They are exempted from all intervention from his part.

He is the judge in the Holy Inquisition, who, without proof, condemned to death by torture those whom he and his peers dislike. He is an ardent Ku-Klux-Klan member, who hung the runaway "nigger" without any trial, he is the slave merchant who transported black Africans to America; he is the one who stalks children and unescorted women in dark alleys.

In his everyday routine, he is a regular wife-beater. Often he beats his children as well, particularly if they try to defend their mother. In some "civilized" parts of our western world, this phenomenon has risen to the dimensions of an epidemic. He applies fervently the Chinese proverb that says that a man must beat his wife three times a day, and if he doesn't know why, the wife does. Women try to protect not only their body from the blows, but their mental sanity from constant abuse. So a new sort of woman emerges; she has persuaded herself that her husband beats her because he loves her. The more he beats, the more he loves, according to the old adage "He who loves chastises". As a matter of fact she has become a masochist. If the husband lets up on the beatings, she is suspicious that he has found somebody else, who loves him better, who is more obedient, who lets herself be beaten more gracefully! In order not to lose her husband's favour, she will repeat, as often as she can take it, the pattern of behaviour that she knows will trigger the abuse. She will be the miserable, dirty, drunken, bad housewife, and he will take off his belt, or clench his fists, and sometimes his teeth: burdened with an undeserving wife, what can he do but teach her to do the right thing? His whole life is a sacrifice. The culture of the poor and miserable goes on, with the occasional black eye and the body covered by make-up.

Body and face make-up is an indispensable item to these families. It is a shame to walk about with the bruises showing what a bad wife the woman is. It is also a shame that she tolerates this degrading behaviour. The whole vicious circle of home violence relies on the principle of the inculpation of the innocent: "You won't tell that I beat you and I won't tell what a lousy wife you are". This method is used when the victim is so powerless that it can turn with immeasurable force against the perpetrator. For example, the uncle who wants to engage his little nephew in a sexual game, will threaten the boy that if he reveals their secret, he (the uncle) will tell the boy's parents that the boy started it. So, it is not rape or molestation, but seduction – or, in legal terms, corruption of a minor – that makes these children suffer these sick situations. Because infantile sexuality is a fact, and curiosity is another characteristic of the young. These two factors combine with the adult's menacing words, and guilt clicks in place. Thus starts the red circle of shame, as the child is persuaded, even by menace – that cannot be proved – to consent to be raped. What the victim of this double atrocity – physical and psychological – does not know is that even if he had tried to resist, he would not have made it. In addition to that, the young person does not know that what the uncle threatened to say, usually and in a normal situation, would not be believed by the young person's parents.

One last remark: only a man can be a rapist, a violator of women and/or other men, as he has the necessary physical strength. A woman can only seduce a man, not only because she is physically weaker, but mostly because the reluctant man, in order to be forced to have sex with her, must be first aroused, he must be tricked, he must be seduced. Only technically can a stronger woman rape a weaker woman or man.

What is the difference between a rapist and a seducer? The former is aroused by the use of physical force, as it is the only thing he has. The latter is a subtler individual, more cerebral, simple violence is not enough for him, because every man is stronger than a woman or a child. He gets high with the use of psychological violence; he persuades his victim to drop its defences, because they are useless against his mental superiority; he wallows in the tears of desperation and humiliation of his victim. Without mercy he will indicate that his desires must be taken as orders, he offers to facilitate things reassuring the victim that soon it will learn to like it, and the sooner it happens, the better. It is an intellectual game of domination, always unilateral and set up.

In our days of mass information, stories of abused women and children often make headlines. Sometimes the older son, for years a witness to the father's brutality, in an attempt to defend either his mother or his brothers and sisters or himself, will kill him and put an end to the family nightmare.

It is worth mentioning the story of a fictitious hero; In an average American middle class family, the father beats the mother since day one. The son grows up seeing the beatings, the crying, the damaged eyes and the broken ribs. In spite of the abuse, the mother is madly in love with her husband. But the son cannot take it any longer, enough is enough. So one day, when his old man is out fishing after having treated his wife as usual, the son takes him by surprise and drowns him in the lake. The authorities suspect what happened, but nobody presses charges against the patricide, everybody had been seeing the mother's black eyes for endless years. But the mother, as soon as she finds out what has happened, throws her son and liberator out of the house, and she refuses to set eyes on him ever again. However, this hatred does not stop her from accepting the money her son sends her through her lawyer. She sees the money as a sort of compensation for the loss she suffered, he as atonement for the murder he committed. The writer is a woman[12]; a woman in a man's world. How exact is her depiction of the female psyche of her times!

Violence is not the only mark of the macho man; tears are another element; or rather their absence. Men do not cry. Almost every father has been trying to persuade his little boy not to cry, not to be a cry-baby. Tears are for weaklings, for women, not for men. Asking little children not to cry is at least cruel, as they cannot always handle speech easily. Crying for children is a way of saying "I'm scared, I'm cold, I'm hungry, it hurts, I don't want to, no". Paternal power does not take 'no' for an answer. A macho man's child obeys his father. Usually the child of a macho father will become an honest and loyal employee, a compromising and tolerant husband, an obedient soldier who will die willingly doing his

---

[12] ANITA BURGH *"Avarice"*, Pan Books, 1994, London, p. 133 and following

duty, in other words, making the vision of his leader come true. But with his own children, he will usually become in his turn a bullying father.

Macho men produce docile children who will become followers, fans, servants and soldiers in suicide missions. But there is an exception to every rule. In some extreme cases, the child will tolerate the father's meanness in order to survive and to become of age. Then he will imitate his father, only to the worse. He may become the psycho serial killer, who hears his father's words echo in his mind. These words, dripping hatred, guide him in his war against humanity. Finally he will find out that no matter how much he hated his oppressive father as a child, he now knows better. Now he loves him, because he realises that the father loved him too, that he always wanted the best for him, that he did what he did for his son's good. If sometimes the father had been too cruel, it was because he wanted to steel the child, he wanted to make a man out of him. Could it be that the father was not so sure of his son's manhood? Could it be that his fears were well-founded? So many lives wasted away, so many souls lost! What a pity!

Man will not accept that he brings about only destruction; or rather that he is the only one to do so. Man has to be tough because woman is tougher. Since the dawn of time, woman has been crushing man. Remember the tales of Samson and Delilah, the Sirens, Circe, Helen of Troy who led two nations in a ten-year bloodshed, or more recently, the Blue Angel. Women have always been able to destroy men. They are cunning and scheming. They ruin a man's reputation, his fortune, his social status; they lead him to suicide. They use artfully sex and their personality, they lead him on; man has no chance. Even a man, who is similar to an ever-enduring rock, can become nothing more than grains of sand in the hands of a woman. Well, "*cherchez la femme*".

The ancient Hellenes used to speak of the three evils in a man's life: Fire, sea and woman.

Oh, men, why the fear, why the insecurity? It is beyond any doubt that man is – at least physically – stronger than women and children. Why has he made them his targets? The woman who is accused of witchcraft, the snivelling son, the amorous and insolent daughter, the lazy wife, the native African whose only weapon is a pathetic bow, all have a muscular system definitely inferior – in the case of the African it is the weapon that is inferior – to that of the man. Why does he have to use violence against them?

All inferior beings terrorize those who are weaker and kneel in front of the stronger. The question is, who is stronger than and superior to man! Only god is above man, his ally and assistant, his creature and creator. God forbid, he cannot antagonise God!

What is more, the weak take advantage of their weakness. So a strong individual must be stronger still in order to put up with the frail and the fragile. Woe on the strong who falls victim to the weakness so dexterously handled by the weak. A strong man cannot lose his precious time trying to explain – tactfully so as not to hurt their feelings – to an idiot that he is an idiot, to a woman that she is a woman and to an effeminate man that he should change his ways. The strong macho man's heart will turn into stone, he will pick up his cudgel and he will beat every idiot's brains into pulp until he makes them see the light, then he will go on to the next case and the next. No rest for the macho man; he has to bring light to the humanity; he has a social mission to accomplish; only an idiot will not understand it.

# THE FEMINIST MOVEMENT

All was well with the macho man and the sharing out of work he had invented: he at work, the wife at home with the children. If it were not for the two world wars, most probably things would have remained the same.

Let us travel back in time, to the 19th century. Man has always been fighting his wars, killing his fellow men, women and children, has discovered new continents and has exterminated entire races. The industrial revolution that originated in the textile industry in England spreads rapidly through out Europe and to other industrial activities as well, changing radically the demographic map of the old continent. Entire villages disappear as the inhabitants move to the big cities that become hydrocephalic, occupying more and more territory of the country, trying to find a place among the factories. Farmers see their land at best expropriated, most often usurped; their helping hands quit the country in search of a job in the factory in the town.

The rustic society becomes rapidly urban. Old customs fall to oblivion, new ones emerge. Woman feels that these profound changes will influence her future and the future of her children. She has to find a way to play a decisive part in the political developments. The suffragettes appear and make the men of their time laugh. They demand the right to vote. Having no arms training, it takes some time, but eventually they gain what they ask. Until late in the 20th century, the western countries, one after the other, accord to women the right to vote. Besides, the time had come.

The intransigent and inflexible morals of the 18th and 19th centuries, as well as the demagogic exploitation of the naïve – and hungry – masses by skilful warmongers, the economic crises that plague Europe and the United States, the miracles of technology thrown in the arsenal of arm dealers, lead to the first and later to the second world war. Never before had humanity lived such a large-scale massacre, never before was the front spanning all five continents, never before extermination of the enemy was so easy, never before were the arms so lethal. The death toll is unbelievable: more than one hundred million victims. Europe is a vast cemetery, almost razed to the ground; in Asia the cities touched by the war are only smoking ruins while thousands of men have perished from the rest of the continents.

The Victorian Puritanism and its morals that imposed the notions of honour, duty, sacrifice in the name of patriotism, obedience to the leader, prepared an eager – and ignorant – human mass to offer the neck to the big butcher of the great ideals. Science has put the finishing touch to the weapons it has been perfecting, but never had had a chance to try. In the First World War it was nerve gas in the trenches. The Second World War presented a huge laboratory for the testing experiments: the entire – fighting – world. The subjects: unsuspecting people. The atomic bombs in Hiroshima and Nagasaki provided numerous cases for the study of the side effects and after-effects of radiation on humans and the environment. The official arm-dealers decided that for a larger target, a larger bomb was necessary; the A-bomb was for small fry. So they placed an order for a bigger one; hence the H-bomb.

In the aftermath of the second war, only women, children and old men were left, watching the dust settle over their ruined cities and tending the disabled and the maimed. Women are obliged to leave their home, or what has been left standing, and search for work, in order to keep alive the children that were spared from the destruction.

The first generation of women who went to work were long past the age of education. So at first they worked as unspecialised workers, mostly in factories. However, having seen how unstable and insecure the man's world is, they sent their daughters to study. From generation to generation, women conquer not only the secondary, but also the high education. The state – for the first time – imposes primary, and later secondary as well – education on all the population, no matter the sex of the children.

In some countries faster and in others more gradually, depending on the hold old customs have on the people, the barrier to education and to professional experience is lifted. Women become bus conductors, accountants, directors, and executive cadres in large multinational companies, lawyers and doctors, scientific researches. They also enter the stadia as athletes. Military academies are no more impregnable fortresses for them, nor is the police force. They also enter politics. They become members of the parliament, ministers, prime ministers, presidents. Finally priesthood is no more taboo, somewhere in England a woman starts saying mass and preaches the word of the Lord.

But equality between the sexes is still far away; women do not get the same salaries as men, although their work is the same, and in some cases superior to that of men. Women prove to be inventive and intuitive, good organisers and hard working. Soon the new super woman appears. She is a successful professional or scientist or employee, a good mother and an exotic wife. Her skills as hostess or as entertainer, in other words as a social being are exceptional. She enters show biz; she even becomes an actress.

Almost every woman has a career, her own income, and her family to look after. She finds out that there is nothing she cannot do. Little by little she sheds her dependency on man. Marriage in not the only means to survival, she can live by her own means. Mothers are not anxious for their daughters to catch a husband, to make a good match. Adultery is no more a crime, punishable by law. If the husband can find himself someone better, let him try his luck. Besides, he has grown flabby around the waist, his hairline is receding, and he has been once again surpassed at work, someone younger got again the long awaited promotion. Let him go in peace. Usually he will not go. He is very proud of – and well settled with – his super wife. He comes back from work and he finds dinner at the table, his clothes clean and ironed, the kids having finished with their homework, the missus helping with the family bills and expenses, what more can he want!

This was the good news for men. Here is the bad news: The feminist movement brought the sexual revolution. Women are now conscious of their body; they demand pleasure from sex, just like men. Wives and one-night-stands alike demand an orgasm, and it is their partner who must provide it. Oh, their poor mother was right, all women are…!

Women demand contraception and the right to discontinue pregnancy not only for medical reasons. The issues of contraception and abortion make or destroy governments, depending on how they are handled. But contraception and abortion deal a heavy blow to the institution of family, the pillar of the man made world. In earlier times, they would not even be considered as issues, they would have been banished from the agenda without any discussion. Not in the late 20th century. Women have become members of the councils and the committees, their voice – and their vote – count. It is a matter of time before all western nations drop all restrictions on these issues.

# THE LIBERATION

The feminist movement brought the long sought liberation. Not the liberation of women from men; as long as women could bear children, they survived somehow. It is man who was finally freed from the legend of the macho man. He threw away the lion hide and the cudgel, and he cried with obvious relief: "At last, I will not have to drink from this cup anymore". It is true that his life has been difficult: always struggling to put – if not the daily cake – at least the daily bread on the table, to fulfil his conjugal duties – so painful after all these years, especially if the wife has put on some weight – often to have a mistress to satisfy as well. Surprisingly, most ex-macho men found out that even without the necessary accessories and the relevant behaviour, they are still men.

Some of them busy themselves with raising their children. They show patience and inventiveness and they help the kids spread their wings and fly, while mothers prefer to have them securely tied to the ground, to avoid all danger. Especially since women left their homes and went to work, the burden of responsibilities weighs them down and their temper is short with the children. Besides, the 9 months that their children spent in their mother's body, make mothers more protective and less imaginative when the security of the children is concerned.

Cake and daily bread apart, it is hard to have always to be the bad guy; the one who beats, who swears, who scares, who prohibits, who punishes, who mangles, who kills or who gives the order to kill. Women, no more protected by male gallantry or sexism or male chauvinism as some of them put it, have to become as tough as they can. Hence, man is not alone anymore. Woman is willing to carry successfully a large part of his burden. Now she can be as mean as a man, in some cases even meaner, and in some other cases, she even likes it. Man can now relax his vigilance, let his defences down, and enjoy a somewhat more peaceful existence, with or without a family.

Changes keep rushing in the established pattern of life. As women advance, so does the sexual revolution. One-night-stands are common, women seek pleasure in and out of matrimony; they become the hunters in the sexual game, while man becomes not the victim, but the trophy. Man is terror-stricken; is this the role he has always wanted, deep down in his heart? Is this why he had always played the macho man, just to exorcize his most secret fears? Now more than ever man is afraid that he is a latent homosexual. In most cases his fears are groundless.

Another consequence of the sexual revolution, equally alarming, is the fact that now women can choose their partner, temporary or permanent. Which means that they criticise; it also means that not all candidates will be accepted; all will be rejected save for one, at least for the time being. To be turned down by a woman, what a shame, how wounded a man's pride can be before he breaks down! *O tempora, o mores!!!* The classic man's world is crumbling further.

While classic men try to recover from the blows inflicted by these changes, homosexuals return with a vengeance. The declaration of the rights of man is freely interpreted, the article about no discriminations is inserted in all constitutions of the western world, and in the late 20th century, homosexuals have found their legal basis: no racial, religious or sexual discriminations. In the same period the first homosexual priest is ordained in England, while the early 21st sees the first mixed marriages blessed by church. The homosexual no long is the black sheep of society. His dignity is restored. Politicians do not care to hide their homosexual tendencies. On the contrary they make them widely known, and they get elected. Is it that the electoral body consists of more homosexuals than one can imagine, or has society become wiser, thus more tolerant?

All the same, in spite of all social progress, some puritan vestiges endure; a politician or a famous business man who is caught with a girlfriend, will have to bear with public outcry, eviction from office or ruin. Elder men who decide to marry younger women see their grown-up children going public with their displeasure at their father's marriage. A man may be a homosexual, but not an adulterer. He must never jeopardise his children's interests by an inopportune alliance. Only half a century ago, the adulterer, or the elder man who entered into matrimony with a younger woman was highly esteemed by his peers, his ego was boosted, he was proud of his uncontested virility, and he was always the first to throw the stone when morals were menaced.

The story of the ex-president of the United States Bill Clinton fits more or less the case; the married man whose – not so – dirty secret is revealed, and he has to apologise publicly, absolution pending for years. In earlier times, his fellow men would have clamoured for more action, he would have been a hero; nobody would have thought of accusing him. It seems that this relic of hypocrisy and Puritanism went out with the 21st century. Future generations could not even imagine such an anachronism, let alone abide by it.

Strangely enough, homosexuals seem the only ones who wish to uphold the traditional institution of marriage and family. They demand the right to adopt children. Most western states do not accept their claim, on the grounds that a child needs both sexes in order to become a well-balanced adult, otherwise it is reared to become a future homosexual. The results in the countries that did finally accept it were dramatic. First of all no marriage lasted for ever, so soon these children were returned to the orphanages or worse the streets, where they presumably came from. In the second place the other children kept ostracizing them as the weirdoes of the company, and third, a large number of them behaved as homosexuals, even if they were not, which, to the eyes of society, amounted to the same as being a homosexual. These children had been predestined to homosexuality ever since they were given up to their adoptive parents.

A homosexual's paradise is the show biz. Singers and actors shed their masculinity in front of their fans (always female) who go frantic with rapture. Manhood and female acceptance and admiration enter a relation in inverse proportion; the less the former, the more the latter. Women worship them. Men disapprove of them, to put it mildly, or despise them, to put it bluntly.

But young boys seem to accept them, to think that they are "cool". Why not grow up to be like them, to have the power and the glory like they do? To have women faint at their feet, screaming their name in adoration, offering their body willingly? The point is, what does an untutored young man do with a proffered female body?

Why do women go ecstatic over homosexuals? Is it that they do not pose a threat to their physical integrity? Women have been fed up with "machismo", they prefer to live without it. A gay man can be a woman's best friend. Let us remember the fabulous George, in the film *"My Best Friend's Wedding"*[13]. No woman could have played the triple role George played successfully for the heroine: he gave her sound advice, he consoled her after she was let down and he played the role of her fiancé in order to see if this would make the other guy jealous. Three friends in one.

But the heaven for gay propaganda is television. Whole series are based on two men, one gay, one straight, and one woman. It is still the old scandalous *ménage a trois,* but the actors and the action have changed: both men are reluctant to enter into a relationship with the woman as the one is gay and the other just unwilling. As the plot goes on, the spectator finds out that the gay is honest, reliable, generous and, strange as it

---

[13] *My Best Friend's Wedding,* 1997. Film. Directed by P. J. HOGAN. Sony Pictures Home Ent. UK

sounds, manly; while the heterosexual is feeble, selfish and abhors all responsibility. Usually the gay in his altruistic aspect will leave all his personal affaires behind – which means that the spectators will rarely see him with his lover – in order to help the woman make the man overcome his reluctance and finally fall in her arms. In these days, no happy ending was possible without a little help from a gay friend.

During the first decade to the 21st, homosexual women also entered television and the cinema. Many were the men who lost their beloved girlfriend or devoted wife to her best girlfriend. Gay women are presented as smart, active, no-nonsense sort of persons who make decisions instantly, are not afraid of anything and of course do not fall prey to the charm of any man.

In these days also, when a still straight woman meets a real, classic man, not necessarily one with the mentality of the cave era, who is charming and interesting, she is afraid that she will be charmed in subjugation once again. She has devised a new trick for this situation. She takes his manly lovemaking, and then challenges him to follow her in the paths of womanhood; she buys him a skirt, female jewellery, and dares him to put them on and take to the streets. If he does not, saying that no man would do such things, she calls him a coward, a gutless, spineless male, whose masculinity she seriously doubts because of his refusal to challenge society for her sake. This is her way to avenge the long slavery of her sex and her reduction to a decorative object, as well as an indirect way to emasculate him. Is it revenge or is it the "penis envy"? Is it an urge to ridicule what no sexual revolution will ever bring her?

Ever since the late 20th century, the female lover has been added to the other three undermining factors of maleness, which have been nature, man himself and his mother.

In the early 21ˢᵗ, a new species of men appears; the metrosexuals. Even football-players who are supposed to be the *machissimi* among men, subscribe to this movement. They are not homosexuals, but as men, they have conquered some of the female taboos: they can pluck their eyebrows, dye their hair, use cosmetics, wear jewellery, shave their body hair, even wear a skirt. Their favourite argument is the advertisement for the whisky "Dewars". "Do you remember the look on the opponents' faces when the calm Scotsmen lifted their kilts?" The answer is, of course, that the Scottish kilt has nothing to do with female garments and effeminate behaviour, while the men of the second millennium are looking for ways to imitate women. Now is the time to wear the mother's – or the wife's – clothes without fear but with a lot of passion.

In the first decade of the same century, homosexuality gets women too. On the one hand the poor females, hungry for a man, are willing to accept any sort of relationship, even a degrading one. They are so eager to do anything the males ask of them! The males on the other hand, fed up with sex-starved women who lay siege to them, propose that the women start kissing each other, they comply, and the rest is easy to guess; one kiss leads to more serious engagements.

It seems that both sexes are happy in the exclusion of each other's company as female homosexuality is dully inserted in the "literature" that is destined for the young people. The older generation is apprehensive and alarmed by the increasing homosexuality among the young. They demand that special measures be taken to the effect of limiting this "moral decease". They predict dangers to the human species as, according to their calculations, births will come to a stop. They are branded as "homophobes" or "gayphobes", assimilated to Cassandra who foresaw only catastrophes and for this reason was imprisoned so that the people of Troy would not be unjustly alarmed, and mankind turns willingly a deaf ear. No more do the passions of the flesh torment the men and women who are content with tepid and harmless liaisons.

# Year 125.897
# Safeland

Masculina closes her book on the "Evolution of human society" and turns on her back, staring at the ceiling. She has read excerpts from this course many times since she enrolled in the Old Times University, and every time she finds something new to fascinate her. Now is the first time she reads it from start to end. The university she has chosen is not a simple educational establishment. It represents the ancient way of learning through knowledge accumulated in books, disks, C.D.s and films, as they were used in schools and faculties until the late 21$^{st}$ century. Actually it is the only university that still functions in the world. Three more that were scattered across the land farther to the south have ceased all classes because they ran out of students. Genetic engineering and safety administration were the only courses that had been taught, until women lost interest.

Classic books and studies became obsolete soon after the 20$^{th}$. Reading was very tiresome; it supposed the recognition of the letters as they travelled through the optical nerve from the eye to the brain. Then the brain had to evoke the images that these words represented. If the notions were simple, it was not so difficult, but if they were abstract or complex, then imagination had to construct the scenes the words implied. Better to use imagery. Practically this meant that it was easier to see a film than to read a book. Journals and newspapers also went rapidly out of fashion. One could watch the news on the television.

Masculina has not many fellow students. People have for centuries preferred the pre-installed memory brain chip that makes old-fashioned education useless. Everything a citizen of today needs to know, is contained in this chip. As a result, schools are almost empty, and professorship is a rare occupation. Rumour has it that the administration will soon close down the schools. However, this will not bring ignorance and illiteracy: the memory brain chip will become genetically installed, so no one will have to worry about it, it will come with the newborn. One of the city's principles is that ethics cannot be enforced by law, they have to be implanted in the individual from birth. In a way, those who work with genetics are the equivalent of the ancient legislators.

She chose this unique way of learning because she herself is unique. She is the last inhabitant on earth who still carries the Y chromosome in her genes. But it has degenerated so much through the eons, that no male indication is evident on her person, save for her purple feeble stubble. She owes the colour to a virtual crossbreeding that took place some millennia ago between some humans and rainbows.

With the book on her side, she drifts slowly to sleep. She wills herself not to dream, because she knows that if she does, sleep will take her through the history course once again. In her dreams she is always the male of the past, participating actively in the events that shaped human history. Human history haunts her, especially the early phases, when war meant body to body combat, and love body to body contact. Her nostrils flare with the unknown smell of freshly spilled blood and charred flesh. She tries to imagine the pain of the wounded and the agony of the dying, the anguish of the bereaved who are left behind. Her torture comes with dawn, when strange sensations creep up from her core to her skin, when she yearns for something unfelt but so familiar, so anciently human.

The first ray of the sun strikes on her suitably positioned mirror and the room is filled with sunlight. In the course of her studies she came upon the Celtic tradition of the Druids and she decided to incorporate this element of sun worship in her own living space; she finds it so fascinating. Although she has no need for machines, her room is full of strange contraptions; she has always been curious about these naïve automations. A toy cross-bow and its arrows lie in a corner on the floor, a percolator is on the table, a sewing machine with a piece of cloth under the needle is on the lower shelf of a glass enclosed book case, a collection of toy cars is on a higher shelf, a perambulator is in another corner, a telescope is on a tripod by the window while on her writing table the screen of a 21st century computer can be seen as well as its keyboard and all the necessary hardware. Actually it is the only piece of ancient machinery that is still working. As for her mirror, she does not use it to watch herself in it as beauty is of no consequence; but it is a perfect alarm clock. All she has to do is to slightly reposition it every night, according to the sun's position on the horizon. In other words, it has to be reset daily.

From the ceiling hang a model aeroplane of a grimy texture and indistinguishable colour with the word AEPOФЛOT scrolled along its flank, and two helicopters, one in khaki, brown and black, the other in black and white with the letters N.Y.P.D. stencilled on it. She is presently trying to unearth a model taxi-cab, preferably one of the yellow ones, and a double-decker red bus, so that her collection will be complete.

On the wall opposite her bed is a huge poster depicting a woman of the ancient times. She has long dark hair, almond brown eyes, high cheekbones and a cherry red inviting mouth. Her body is a study in curves. Her breasts are voluptuous but firm, her waist is so slim that a single arm could encircle it, her hips are round and her legs long and smooth. She is tanned and her skin looks so smooth, she would love to touch – caress – it. She is in a certain state of undress as few undergarments still cling to her heavenly body. High on her right thigh is an oily smudge that resembles a fingerprint. She seems to be in a euphoric state and to be on the lookout for someone to share it. Underneath the photo are words and numbers. Masculina's researches have revealed that the anonymous woman is a model posing as a stripper, and pretending to be in a sexy mood, in order to keep the customers satisfied. The picture is a page torn from a nude calendar that used to decorate walls in places where lots of men would come together, usually after physical exertion, like locker rooms. The oily smudge however suggests that it originally hung in a garage, where cars – those obsolete individual transportation means – were repaired mainly by men.

At first, Masculina was stricken by the beauty of the creature. She could not take her eyes from the ancient young woman. Not only the physical appearance puzzled her, she could not believe that once upon a time women were shaped like this. But there was also another quality that escaped all known definition; it was lust, sexual, carnal lust. She would lie in her bed and gaze straight into the woman's eyes while her mind would wander, and all the strange feelings would shatter her peace of mind. However, after the initial fascination wore away, she would avert her eyes from the photo. She preferred not to provoke the torturous sensations by looking at the poster. Besides she was purely jealous, not only of the woman, but of the whole lost and irretrievable era.

Smaller pictures, framed or not, of earlier human activities are scattered around the room; here a couple in the ceremonial garb of marriage, looking lovingly into each other's eyes, there a grainy photo of a black woman in labour in an operating room, on another shelf the image of a blond, blue eyed baby taken from an advertisement for baby food as it stares happily, and on the back of the door a large picture of the Chinese students demonstrating in Tien Ah Mehn Square, a few minutes before they were gunned down by the riot police. Another poster of smaller dimensions is tacked on the wall next to the eastern window, where a blond young man with green eyes, muscles rippling, lies nonchalantly on a chair. "I would be him and she would be mine", Masculina used to muse, usually before she drifted off to sleep.

Finally, on the wall behind her bed rest, a small highly polished ebony crucifixion is tacked, as she has seen in many ancient movies. "Imagine", she says to herself, "their God sent his son among men, and they crucified him. Then, they made the crucifixion a symbol of their faith. Probably because they did not wish to forget how painful is the way that leads to the kingdom of heaven". She has no way of knowing that the cross was preferred because it trapped the individual into misery and guilt, the only escape being obedience to the church, hoping for a release in the after-world as a well deserved reward.

The members of the High Council were initially shocked with the idea that all this stuff from the past would be proudly exposed to the peaceful Safelanders. "Make her take them down and return all of them to the storehouses" said the youngest of the officers. "No, let her have them and show them around. She will take them down one day all by herself, mark my words" said an elderly woman with a soft, kind voice. It was her advice that the Council followed, only to see it come true many years later.

From the literature Masculina has read, she is aware of the super-natural world of the ancient people, which existed in parallel lines with the natural and the spiritual one. Ghosts came back to tend to business that an untimely death left unfinished, they haunted the place where they gave up the spirit and they avenged their death – or at least they tried to. Vampires lived off the living, banshees and trolls and werewolves tormented them, ghouls and zombies were a very dark side of human nature, fairies and elves and gnomes and guardian angels protected or mislead unsuspecting humans. "You name it, they had it", she mumbles as she is slowly emerging from the depths of her sleep, as her dreams have been, once again, filled with such creatures. "Imaginary creatures" she corrects herself. "Wonderful", she goes on, "now you talk to yourself, what will come next?" "Lonelyyyy, you're so lonelyyyy" a little sing-song voice whispers inside her head. "Shut up!" she hisses, "I have my friends, and most of all I have Felina". "Sure, you have a fulfilling relationship, this is why you talk to yourself". She chooses to ignore this tiny but all the same insistent voice, because dawn is already chasing away the shadows in her garden.

She comes fully awake, and her mind is troubled. No matter how hard she willed herself not to dream, she did not make it. Sensations have once again been harassing her, tearing the fabric of her sleep to pitiful rags. And if this is not enough, now she has started hearing voices in her sleep and, what is worse, answering back. She picks up her book and goes to sit in the garden.

This part of the planet has been preserved as it was before the nuclear strike that erupted when, late in the third millennium, the president – it is presumed it was a man among the few that were left – of a mini-state went trigger happy, and three quarters of the earth became uninhabitable and 7 billion people were instantly vaporised. The only survivors – at the first calculations only a couple of million and most of them women but as it turned out they were even less – were the inhabitants of a vast plain, the only place that the wrath of the imbeciles had left unscathed. Here the Engineers built a temperate zone and stabilised a mild climate. Soil was brought from the ocean bed where radiation had not penetrated, and genetically programmed crops were planted. These crops needed no tending, no care at all; they just bloomed from the same old roots, ready for harvest, every trimester.

Masculina has designed and built this unique garden herself. After a thorough research in the museum archives and warehouses, she managed to locate seeds of pear trees, lemon trees, rose bushes and heliotropes. The genetic code of these seeds has not been tampered with, and their bloom follows the old natural annual cycle. Spring is in the air and the rose bush is budding, while the scent of the lemon tree flowers brings a sense of innocent and trusting childhood, although she cannot locate the source of the feeling. Her garden is unique in the city, just like her. People do not trust her, and she is better off alone. In this colourless, tasteless and odourless world, her garden provides the only splash of colour, the only whiff of fragrance and her kitchen the only food that does not taste like straw.

The only colours that the authorities recognise and which can be legitimately worn by the inhabitants are brown and grey in all their hues. Red and yellow and turquoise and orange and mauve were regarded as garish and people were discreetly advised to avoid them at all costs. White was associated with earlier notions of purity, virginity and the ceremony of marriage, while black invoked evil and mourning, all of them imposed by male rule in order to control women, so neither was favoured. Of course the sky and the sea are blue, the trees – necessary for the oxygen – are green but these are the colours of nature. But flowers are useless, so there are no flowers in the land other than those in Masculina's garden.

As for the nutritional habits of the population, breakfast, lunch, dinner and supper all come in the form of small slabs of compressed and chemically enriched cereals that taste like straw. This diet eliminated the problem of obesity that had so much tormented the earlier populations of the rich western countries. The lack of flowers also meant no odours and the lack of garbage no stench either.

Book in hand, she goes back to her reading of the night before.

* * *

Back in the early 21$^{st}$ century, people were still unaware that society was gradually turning back to its former matriarchal form. No bloodshed has been necessary; no riots, no pompous slogans; the ferocious enemy has willingly and unknowingly capitulated. Homosexuals are once again accepted into society as equals because women, unlike men, tend to protect themselves and those who resemble them, such as the homosexuals because they pose no threat. Homosexual men are not as aggressive as the heterosexuals. Thus they are safer, if not as sexual mates, at least as members of the same society. Besides, the participation of women in politics has rendered society more sensitive to extra-ordinary people.

Bisexuals are not *en vogue* any more, it is considered immoral to have the best of the two worlds. One should always chose his preferred sex and stick to it by showing loyalty. Passing from men to women and vice versa showed a weakness in character, an emotional instability, so that bisexuals are considered unreliable.

Female homosexuality has not modified seriously the spirit of women. Already since the previous century they had showed signs of aggressiveness, savagery and competitiveness, and as centuries turned into centuries, women rationalised violence: it would be used strictly for defending the feebler. It was exactly the same pretext men had used in order to justify violence. How accommodating!

At the same time, men who in the times of machismo were considered as second rate males because they were mild and civilised in their ways, now enjoy a tremendous success. Women adore these quiet, home-loving men, who do not mind staying at home and preparing dinner for their beloved who comes back from a hard day at work. Men who cook are trendy, actually cooking becomes one of their assets, a *sine qua non*, while younger women consciously ignore everything about cooking; actually the less they know about this art, the sexier and most desirable they are.

In other words, man and woman are not contained within the limits that the man-made society has imposed on them, the roles are interchangeable; the objective becomes a companionable and less strenuous life.

It sounds ideal. But it does not mean that all problems have been eliminated from the relationship between the sexes.

# THE UNISEX TREND
## *Year 125.897, Safeland*

At a time when all established values are disputed and challenged, people decided to do away with all differentiation, in the name of equality. In practice it meant that women threw away their high-heeled pumps, their dresses with the nipped waist, they cut their hair short, and elegance soon became as out-dated as the medieval corsets. Men in their turn tint their hair and let it grow, unkempt and dishevelled; they wear the same eponymous, expensive and gross garments. It is difficult to tell a man from a woman, particularly among the young. It is true that the younger the individuals, the less are their differences. At the time of birth, only their genitals distinguish them. As they grow older, each child becomes different from the other, not only because of its sex, but also because of its genes and its environment.

Childhood constitutes a more or less homogenous age; all children, boys and girls, black, white and yellow, wish to be fed, to be kept warm and clean. They all want to feel loved, hugged and held and cuddled. Later, they wish to play, and to get to know themselves. Then it is the world they want to be acquainted with. At this point the differences appear, and grow into gaps, according to who their teacher is and what he teaches them, as it is different education and different upbringing that breed different points of view.

At this era people have stretched the age boundaries of childhood. They wish to remain undistinguishable – in other words irresponsible – as long as possible. Young men and women wear the same clothes, listen to the same music, and all speak English, the international language. Internationalism helps spread the same habits all over the globe, while the same movies are simultaneously projected in all major cities. The youth of New York and San Francisco share their heroes with the youth in London, Paris, Beijing, Tokyo and Moscow, also Hanoi, Delhi and Rio de Janeiro. Western eating habits have also touched all the rich capitals, adding to the local food varieties the American hamburger with French fries on the side and the omnipresent soda drink to the wineries of the world. This uniformity in food has largely contributed to the elimination of skin hues, height and body structure differences.

It is not only in outer appearance that young people avoid maturity, differentiation and responsibilities. It is also in their inner life that they remain infants: The family home remains their home as long as possible, and parents and their forty year-old children are happy together under the same roof. The sexual mates come and go but the nucleus of the family remains unbroken, and, more often than not, sterile. In case that any new children should be added, they are part of their parent's family.

In order to attain total uniformity, all extremes must be discarded. No extreme beauty in either men or women, no exceptional talent to be distinguished by. In advertisements models are unkempt, colourless, tasteless and odourless: ordinary people, like us. In these days, marketing experts did not attempt to temp consumers through the beauty associated with models and products. The message was that you too, ordinary though you are, even ugly, can enjoy this or that product. You don't have to be better than you really are, our product is for you, man and woman of no distinction. Now love and happiness through thoughtless consumerism, are addressed to all people.

But do ever people stop dreaming of princes and princesses? No, because the simple and the ordinary are always the others, **we** are always special. Women will still dream of prince Charming, so that their children will be special. Beasts will always be on the look out for the Beauty. If we accept that we are all common people, no prince Charming and no

Beauty, love loses all interest. Nobody wants to fall in love with a common man or an ugly woman. And when love loses all interest, people find other things to bide their time.

The sexual revolution brought an excessive supply / offer of women. But an excessive supply brings down the prices and diminishes demand; in other words it diminishes desirability. When in earlier times men who wanted to have sex were obliged either to turn to a prostitute or to marry, or at least to enter into a long engagement full of lies and compromises, where marriage was eventually inevitable, now they have to do nothing. Actually women offer themselves up for free, no strings attached. Besides, he does not have to look for his own Beauty, all women are beautiful thanks to modern cosmetology and plastic surgery. It is getting boring!

However, this situation did not last long. At first women, drunk with freedom went with all men. Soon things changed, and women started dreaming again. Not of families and children, of life-lasting relations, of bellies blemished with stretch marks and sleepless white nights, but of a one-night-stand, provided that their partner would be The man. He had to be famous, a celebrity, also handsome, while wealth was a definite plus. Inner qualities such as education, honour, understanding, were of no consequence.

The most important factor in the formation of new morality, seems to be entertainment. Technology has enriched this field considerably. Let us consider that in the past, man rose and slept with the sun. There was no electricity, and the only thing a couple could do after sundown was to have sex. It also generated warmth, indispensable in the cold winter nights. Contraception was prohibited by church and besides life was cheap, it required no special care. The multitude of children born to a homestead year in, year out, was, according to an old French proverb, the poor man's riches.

Couples of the late 20<sup>th</sup> century and afterwards, have had other options and other priorities. If a day's hard work has not exhausted them completely, they may watch T.V., go to the movies or the theatre, have dinner with friends, pursue one of their hobbies, go dancing, have a quarrel or do some house chores. In the wee hours of the morning they would usually call it a day. "Let's get some sleep darling, sex can wait. When was it the last time we made it, do you remember, because I, frankly, don't".

Entertainment enters not only the individual's life, but also its psyche. Despite the etymology which means "being among others", modern entertainment cultivates isolation. The young walk around – or take the buses, trains and the metro – with walkmans plugged in their ears, cut off from their environment. In their own cars and apartments, the volume of music is unbearably high. In movie theatres, the Dolby Surround system makes the spectators participate in the action on the screen; noises can be heard and thuds felt through the floor and the walls. Even smells seep in the theatre, making the film more realistic. In this way, contemporary people have no need of chemicals to travel in other worlds; modern technology takes them to places they have never been, without any harm and with no side effects.

If they go to a club or a disco, the music is so loud that no communication is possible. People dance on the stage but they dance alone, everyone in his own reveries. When they go to concerts, again the music monopolizes their attention; they are not permitted even to whisper to their neighbour, music on the stage is so loud it absorbs all the other elements. Is this isolating fun the result of a situation where people have nothing to say to each other, or, to the contrary, is it what truly caused the "isolation in the crowd" phenomenon?

In the past it was ignorance that kept people quiet – they did not know what to say. In these days, it is the sound. When you listen to deafening music, you cannot communicate your feelings, and what is more, you cannot criticize. Karl Marx, inventor of communism back in the 19th century, used to say that religion was the opium of the masses. However, the philosopher, highlighting the soporific influence church had upon the individuals, has failed to discern the simultaneous stimulating quality of religion, as was the case of the crusades or the imperialistic dogma of the Muslims, when the faithful become aggressive against the infidels and commit hideous atrocities, each in the name of their faith.

Next century brought football that kept people happy, the equivalent of the Roman "bread and spectacles". As sociology advances, it becomes clear that peace cannot be imposed either by law or by force. The ideal way to do it would be through education. It would take scores of generations, but finally people would learn to respect human rights, and to live in free societies. But as free public education has not been viable in most countries as the populace grew in numbers, other, more insidious and more efficient ways had to be researched. For example, by raising the decibels, people learn to keep quiet and listen. That is, people learn to accept whatever comes from higher above (the loudspeakers, the authorities). They learn to be obedient and indifferent. By keeping quiet, language declines and abstract nouns become redundant. Words like freedom, reason, treason, love, become pointless. By not using them, people stop thinking about them: they forget them. Familiar, isn't it? *1984*, George Orwell.[14]

No oppression, no commands issued, no special legislation. So smooth, so cunning, so satanic!

Morals of the early third millennium are so different from those of the first two. A new hierarchy of priorities arises. In the civilized western

---

[14] ORWELL George, *Nineteen eighty four*, Longman Publications, 1983.

world, sex has long ago lost its predominant place in the life of humankind. Hence the acute demographic problem that plagues the planet, and the European countries in particular. For some time it seems that at least the Asian countries will go on producing babies. But as civilization, technology and western culture and customs reaches and embraces them, they too reduce activities which result in child bearing. As a consequence, the third millennium finds mankind severely declining as its active elements are not renewed at the same rate as they expire. Young people grow old and die without leaving sufficient children behind. It is only to be expected, as men become more and more homosexual, and all the rest of men and women alike turn asexual.

From a philosophical point of view, the individualism that appeared so timidly with the French revolution of 1789 and the Declaration of human rights, finds now its absolute application – to the point of perversity. Particularly among the young, nothing matters more than their petty comfort and well-being. All the high ideals such as patriotism, humanism or environmentalism of the past have fallen prey to oblivion. Men and women care only for themselves.

From a practical standpoint, the states of providence that thrived in Europe and most of the civilised world in the 20th century, can not afford to continue providing for their citizens any more, as the old in need of medication keep living longer and longer, while the input of fresh people is reduced to a trickle. As a result, if a couple decides to raise a family, the entire economic burden – which is considerable – falls solely on their shoulders. A few centuries later, no more subsidies are voted by the parliaments, all special allocations from the state are revoked.

Children do not need only money to grow up. They also need care and time. Time is as precious as money. Who will sacrifice his time for the children's sake? Who will put his career aside to plunge into diapers, baby food and toilet training? People do not need their children any more in order to secure some help in their old days. They have their job, their savings, their retirement plan and their medi-care system. Why go into all this trouble? Why should the woman get pregnant and suffer all the inconveniences it entails, such as morning sickness, overweight, stretch marks, breast feeding? Why should the father stay at home with the infant, while he could still be out there in the rat-race, making money? To make a long story short, people do not need children to look after them; their money will buy them as much care as they need.

Money has always been the power that made the world go round. Particularly after the Second World War, when growth after the destruction was riotous, and wealth easily accessible, man became *homo economicus*, and later he became simply a consumer. All that is expensive becomes a status symbol, so men and women have to be able to afford it, in order to be admitted into higher circles, because man is still a sociable being, he simply does not communicate any more. But he consumes. Alone or in company, man eats up food, energy (petrol, gas,) and natural resources (water). Human waste in the U.S.A., if dumped into the Pacific ocean, would fill it up, and with time, would form mountains and valleys.

The original consumer was the woman. Always in the quest for beauty and eternal youth, so that she could keep her man, she would buy primitive jewels, cosmetics and cloth to make new garments. Industry and technology brought forth numerous products that would help her in her struggle against time. But as society changed, man entered commerce, not only as producer and worker, as formerly, but as a customer as well. Cars and yachts, sports equipment, jewellery and art become his targets, while he also purchases cosmetics specially designed for him. As for the woman consumer, no matter how society has changed, and takes into consideration education and professional accomplishments, her number one target remains the beauty industry. As the time goes by, people, men and women, need to be accepted by their superiors, acknowledged by their peers, and coveted by their inferiors, so they simply keep buying.

Purchase is the surest way to acquire love, esteem and entry. Consumers of the late 20ᵗʰ may be assimilated to a herd of irresolute beings – whose motto is "I consume, therefore I exist" – being led to stampede-like shopping sprees, simply because fashion imposes this or that product. Needless to say that the only products that are on sale are those that are fashionable. Should someone wish for something that is out-dated, only chance may bring it his or her way. On the contrary, once a product is fashionable, it can be found in all shopping areas, only prices change. As everybody struggles to buy it, it becomes a must. In the end, no matter the social or the economic status, everybody proudly shows off the priceless acquisition. Finally consumerism has turned against its prime objective, which was the establishment of social barriers. Now everybody finds a way – over indebted credit cards, consumers' loans and periodical instalments – to have what all the others have. Consumerism has finally brought down all apparent barriers among the classes. Only the truly penniless remain outside the commerce cycle. And they are numerous.

The equalization of the two sexes into one and asexual goes beyond the level of appearances; it goes deeper. It shows that, when a creature of nature conquers reason, it may well escape from its biological boundaries and its destiny and soar to the sky, or plunge to hell if it chooses to abuse or to ignore its capabilities. In the case of the human species, nature made woman for procreation purposes, and man to add some spice to life and support her. Then, man conquered reason and speech. For millennia he excluded woman from his conquests. Until, overcome by aggressiveness, his sole power, he lost all control and nearly led humanity to extinction. The scales tipped over, he was forced to let woman enter dynamically his world. In her turn, she finds out that there is nothing she cannot do and she wants revenge. She intimidates man; she feminises him to make sure that no macho man will be resurrected from the past to threaten her future.

She helps him in the management of everyday life, but also in the management of the world. It is a time of perpetual experimentation for her, when old values are continuously revised; the obsolete ones are abolished, often with no new ones to take their place.

The human being of the late 20th refuses to adhere to the labels society made up. It is man or woman or whatever else, without predetermined roles, without different behaviour patterns. Young women, in order to prove their equality with men, their sameness, smoke, drink and swear heavily. This is mimicry of the lower elements which can be easily copied. Usually individuals with low self-esteem and with an inferiority complex towards those they imitate adopt this behaviour.

It would be unfair to insist on the negative side of equalization. There is also a sunny side. This phenomenon shows a tendency to reconciliation. "We are not enemies any more, we are alike, there is nothing that can come between us". Men and women demonstrate that they do not care to be a couple any more, as something more profound binds them: they are allies and fellow warriors in the struggle against ignorance and vanity that have made the future of our planet uncertain.

Nothing is to be gained by holding men responsible for the enormous damage to the environment. Nothing is to be gained either if men accept their responsibility.

Because men took charge of the affairs of the world, though arbitrarily, they cannot be held responsible forever. Particularly if their policy is ineffective or, worse still, destructive. Together, men and women, must keep up the fight for the preservation of human life. Women must put aside all feelings of vengeance, wilful weakness and refusal of responsibility. If the damage to our planet is still reversible, only co-operation between the sexes will save it.

\* \* \*

Masculina sighs and puts the book down, the authors of this work were too close to the era and they were not able to see things clearly. "Humans", she thinks to herself. "Always eager to put the blame on the other, the gypsy, the Jew, the homosexual, the political opponent." People of such an early time held the homosexuals responsible for the degeneration of the social life. And those who came after them did not bother to put things right. Actually, the homosexuals were the only ones who, in their love affairs, maintained the duality of the sexes; one was the man and the other was the woman, albeit their external appearance told a different story.

On the contrary, it was the heterosexuals who did nothing to preserve this duality, it was them who let the two sexes merge into one. When nature made humans man and woman, each sex was assigned a different mission: the male was meant to impregnate as many women as possible, hence the male polygamy that later women have so fiercely fought against, and the female had to bear as many children as the ova in her ovaries. Reason came and sentiments between the sexes arose. Observation with reason showed that endogamy produced defective children, so siblings should not have children. Sentiments on the other hand became complicated with time: love, possessiveness, jealousy, loyalty would torment the poor humans and turned the most highly praised feeling, love into a nightmare that led quite a few people to suicide or to murder. However, it seems that during the early matriarchal times, children and men did not belong to anyone.

When men took the power in their hands, women had to belong to their husbands and female adultery was severely punished in all political and religious regimes. In some parts of the world they said that it is the woman who keeps the family together (if she abstains from cheating on her husband) by turning a blind eye to her husband's womanizing, because, after all, he is only obeying to his natural mission. If she sticks to her own charges, which are the children, everything will be fine. So she is by nature monogamous, as her only concern is to find the perfect male to father her children. And when she finds him, she wants him to stay close, to help with the upbringing of the little ones, who really need both of their parents. Besides, in the past, after the first child, the woman was not marketable any more as her body had been irreparably disfigured. Who would stay with her to go on with the rest of the children she had to carry if not the first, the chosen one?

Yet, in the early 21st century humans overcame their nature: men got tired of sniffing at the hems of the women's skirts, and women got fed up with bearing children, for the reasons exposed above. Both retired to asexual, solitary lives, and the female being stronger, they drifted towards a monosexual, effeminate world and passed from male polygamy and female monogamy, to total agamy. While this was happening with the heterosexuals, only the homosexuals still had an active sexual life, where both sexes were represented.

As for the ecological concerns of these primitive people, Masculina knows that the damage was irreversible, but humans adapt to everything. Besides, nature, the first and ultimate creator, is tenacious and manages to outlive all destruction caused by its creatures.

Deeply troubled by her own conclusions, she goes back to her book.

* * *

# EVOLUTION AND DEGENERATION OF Y
## *2003-2679-3815-3848-125.897-296.561, Safeland*

It was in the year 2003 that scientists from the Oxford University announced to the world that the Y chromosome shows signs of degeneration, and some thousands of years later it is quite possible that males will have been extinct. The issue here is not the biological and genetic development of Y, but the evolution of society.

* * *

Masculina raises her eyes from the page as a shadow falls across it. It is her special friend, Felina, who comes to study together. Actually, it was Felina and the feelings she awoke in Masculina, that made the latter look into the past for explanations.

The deeply hidden and almost completely emasculated man that lay dormant in her – the High Council gave her this name, among other reasons, in order to exorcise euphemistically the evil male element – made her loins stir uncomfortably at the sight of her fellow woman. Amazingly, the feelings were mutual. When their eyes locked, it was like sparks flying. This totally unexpected feeling peeled away the layers of skin that hid all traces of features and made them all look alike. Looking at Felina, Mascoulina would see a mildly freckled face crowned by a red mane that, according to the angle of light varied from tawny to copper with a pair of soft hazel eyes which shone mischievously on the world and a mouth she longed to kiss. The curves were all in the right places but it was difficult to tell if they were full or not quite so. Respectively, those hazel eyes, when focused on Masculina, detected the man underneath with his fair hair and skin and steel blue eyes and the fully muscular body. When they touched, at first accidentally and later on purpose, they felt melting inside. But their bodies were not adjusted to love-making, evolution had seen to it, so that what was never used any more was soon erased, pending of course, further developments.

Soon the High Council got wind of the scandalous affaire. However they decided to leave the couple alone, a history of more than a hundred millennia has taught them that eventually violence hurts the one who uses it. Victims become martyrs and martyrs bring turbulence, they disrupt the peace, they breed revolution through followers and mimicry, and eventually they bring back violence. The authorities could not afford that. They simply showed to the rest of the women that they were not favourable to the situation. But they were to be left alone. Masculina's eventual natural death would bring a natural end to all this. The perilous one-legged equilibrium would be re-established.

Masculina, an imperfect creature, thankfully the last one on earth, would not be able to live as long as the others. All the memories of her male collective memory, all the sentiments – such a useless thing – would wear her down sooner than the usual average of 200 years that was expected of a woman. Her recent lab tests showed that she had no more that 50 years.

Besides, the citizens of Safeland – a name that showed that safety was guaranteed to all its inhabitants, at the opposite of the Old World, where men were incapable of securing nothing but chaos and massacre – had never sympathised with Masculina's double sexuality, and never would in the future. So prudence dictated discreet indignation.

Safelanders could not tolerate their single minimal sexuality, let alone a double one. Sex has been for ages totally forgotten as a means of procreation. Anyone who wished to know how the Old People multiplied, had to search in the dusty volumes of the library of the Old

Times University. The material was sufficient: there were sketches, photos, biological explications taking into consideration the hormones chemistry, erotic literature, even pornographic video tapes and films. But moderns failed to comprehend the mysterious ways in which two – or more – bodies reached ecstatic pleasure. As a matter of fact, the language of the Safelanders had no definition for "ecstatic pleasure". Soon all interest vanished, the whole issue of sex being discarded as "a chemical weakness, an imperfection in the human organism of the ancients".

However, some of the researchers in the Library took special care to hide the mixed emotions their wanderings had produced: revulsion and at the same time longing, curiosity and wonder, an awakening and at the same time a little death. They all enrolled at the History Department of the University, as they wished to find out everything about the context into which Old People fell in love. The students – few that they were – all were excited by Masculina, she was the last link to the past. An intellectual elite was formed round the "last Y", as they jokingly called her. The authorities kept a discreet tab on all of them.

To their surprise the two friends who were at the core of this elite found out that soon after they started courting and studying together, the perception they had of their fellows, friends and strangers alike, changed drastically. Neither the uniformity of garment nor the uniqueness in appearance could hide anymore the women they would have been. Their professor became a fine featured slender negress, the officer who lived two blocks from the Old Times university looked to them like an embittered spinster, the rest of their friends took on the various appearances and the colours of the past. For them, the humans that surrounded them were now distinct and different from each other. But this new ability would be considered a breach of one of the founding principles of their land, the principle of absolute equality, so they wisely decided to keep it from the authorities.

\* \* \*

In the unique garden the two friends sit side by side. They have to discuss the free topic of an essay their professor assigned to them for the end of the term. They have decided to present an imaginary world, where woman will have perished, and man alone will exist and rule. It will be interesting to speculate how it will end. Masculina will contribute her maleness to the story, Felina will furnish the female aspects.

Professor Femella was thrilled. And at the same time scared out of her wits. What if the High Council finds out about the essay? What if she is accused of treason? Of instigating trouble among the students with "forbidden material from the past"? She knows that she is in no danger of physical termination. But she may well be discharged from her office, and publicly denounced as an "agent of the enemy". Although women are not particularly communicative any more – gone are the days of happy gossip over the phone, or at the hairdresser's salon – and they do not seek each other's company, their disdain can be very clear to the unfortunate who is still haunted by men, and not prudent enough to hide it.

\* \* \*

"Do you remember how it all ends?" asks Felina. "I mean in the book."

"Definitely I do. Who wouldn't?" replies Masculina.

"It's unbelievable. Men and women have been so careless, so frivolous. They let it all go down the drain".

"Come on, stop snivelling, let's get on with our reading, we have to make sure that we have the facts straight. Let's recap, from the time woman entered the arena of earning a living outside her home, till the end of the era."

\* \* \*

Women assume new roles, and men leave behind their traditional ones to stay at home and raise the children. This is true of those who still stick to the old pattern of living in the family circle. More children are born out of the blessings of the church and are raised by a single parent, sometimes the mother, sometimes the father. New religions and cults appear, all short-lived with a limited number of followers. It is the old desire to belong somewhere, to share the same beliefs and principles. The phenomenon grows stronger as family grows fainter.

Woman, delirious with her newly acquired power, does not know what she really wants. Her actions contradict her wishes, as she leads man to effeminate ways and he follows willingly, only to suddenly find out to her dismay that there are no more men left. And there is no macho man around to console her.

Yet, another point of view must be explored: It is men who claim that there are no more real men left, in order to keep the woman of their heart satisfied with the man she has got, so that she may stop looking around. Men keep always undermining each other, they do not hesitate to slander their own sex. It seems that competition is too tough, as less masculine men have now entered the contest for the favours of a woman. No solidarity can be found among men. They do not support their cause; they accuse each other of inadequate maleness!

Women who want a real man, in the tradition of the medieval knights, are obliged to look among older men, who refuse to wear skirts and earrings, but who do not grab the woman by the hair to drag her to their lair. It is not the lure of the silver-grey temples that attracts younger women to older men, neither their supposed superior experience in love making, nor the tolerance that a wiser person will show to the frivolousness of a younger one. It is simply the manly qualities that younger men lack.

This should have been a transitory phase, where capabilities would be explored from both sides. Women should have soon – the planet is running out of time – recovered from the state of confusion and helped men get to their feet. Besides, the dilemma between the man in the lion hide who speaks with his fists and the one who wears skirts and dyes his hair is false. It takes two extreme cases and leaves out the essence, which is that men and women may yet find harmony in living together, may thrive in the solidarity of fighting together for the survival of their habitat.

This goal would have been attained had they discarded all that separated them in the past, had they invented new values, compatible with them and with their environment. Repressed emotions of thousands of years constitute an insurmountable obstacle to the victorious march to the future. This would be the time – for women in particular – to pursue real emancipation from feelings of inferiority and superiority, subordination, tolerance, forbearance and revenge. Female memory should be purged of all resentment.

It is already evident that extinction is waiting for man, at the next bend of the road. He does not resist this feminisation that woman has started. He identifies himself with her, at least to the extent that he can.

Only some older men resist this *vogue,* which threatens to drown the world. They were born men and they will die men. Their passionate hatred for women drives them to extremities. They despise all women, they refuse even to negotiate with them, not even for the sake of those to be born. For them, women are the bearers of all evil, they are stupid and unclean, all they do is sow confusion to male minds. Although old age finds them misogynists, in their youth they had been ardent lovers of "the fair sex", having loved their mother's friends and those of their wives. Nothing could keep them away from other women's skirts. Victims of mothers, grand-mothers, wives, mistresses and daughters – whom they never really understood, no matter how much they claimed they loved them – they finally give vent to the oppression they suffered in their beloved's hands. They also despise men who trust women, as effeminate, thoughtless and useless. For them, the whole human species is useless and does not deserve to be saved from its folly. Maybe this is why they do nothing to put sense in human minds. Could it be that a misogynist is either a misanthrope or a homosexual?

Woman may be vengeful, but this may not be the only factor that guides her in her unpredictable ways: Most probably she fears that the planet, and humankind with it, is beyond salvation, no matter what she does; as a result the continuity of life does not concern her any more. Deprived of her natural reason for living, she unleashes her power with no restraints, she lets her biological clock run wild, destabilising everything in her wake.

Contrary to earlier predictions that warned of overpopulation of the planet, births diminish with each generation. Men and women enjoy their freedom, happy and carefree.

In our opinion, life without men will mean extinction of humankind, no life at all. Is this what we really want?

\* \* \*

Masculina passes the book to the hands of her friend, as she has finished with it. She knows that it has been written in the year 2679. "Look" cries her friend, "Let's try to find if the authors have been men or women". She groans inwardly but she goes along with her friend's whims. She knows that their fellow-women can be sillier than Felina. "O.K., you go first". "Right, Dimitris François de Ville. Dimitra was a goddess of some sort, wasn't she?" "Yes, so this must be a man, and a French with Greek blood if the name and surname are to be taken into consideration. Who is next? Maria Vasilievna Kulagina. Too many 'a's, it is definitely a she. From a Slavic state. Maria was mother of god if my memory does not fail me. Next! Alberto Pesante, definitely a man and almost certainly Italian. Who is last?" "Lu Chi Minch". "The name, no doubt, is Chinese, but as to the sex, I cannot tell".

As Felina goes back to her reading, Masculina thinks of the future the authors of this book did not know and so much feared.

* * *

In order to keep the war machine going, the super powers invented the cold war in the second half of the 20th century, where fear for a nuclear holocaust held back the two protagonists from pressing the red button. The planet was holding its breath for almost fifty years, until eventually one of the giants collapsed. The Soviet Union could not resist the capitalist system any longer. The secret alliance formed by political and ecclesiastic forces was the external factor while the inherent weakness of a regime that was fake combined and in the year 1989, the communist empire finally succumbed. The most celebrated fact of the time was the fall of the wall of Berlin, or the wall of shame. It is said that Berliners took it down brick by brick. Only one super power was left, the United States of America. But not for long.

China emerged, out of the gloom of its century old isolation, resplendent in cheap production because of cheap labour and gathered in her hands the economic reins. But the regression that followed this spell of economic growth found the country unprepared. Besides, handling the world trade was a very heavy load for a country that had no tradition in the capitalist system. When China came down, she brought the whole world down with her. After the cosmic economic breakdown of the 34th century, no more super powers were left to claim the leadership of the planet.

Arms trade – probably the most profitable – was kept up by supporting and encouraging rebellions in underdeveloped countries. Several wars about possession of the mineral resources of the East would erupt from time to time, under the mask, of course of a fight to bring democracy to the oppressed populations. Water sources have also been much claimed and fought over, as potable water became rare with each degree the temperature of the surface of the earth rose. Man has had the chance to show his brutality in these wars once again, where torture was freely applied, civilians were slaughtered and prisoners of war treated like slaves or executed on the spot, despite the series of the Geneva Conventions that had originally been signed by the Red Cross in 1864[15].

Male population was divided in two: the smaller portion included the soldiers, mercenaries and military officials, who designed and executed these wars. All the others, gradually became homosexuals or totally asexual. Women were similarly affected, as the lack of men brought the loss of interest in sex and family. Most women refused to go through the "primitive ritual" of insemination, pregnancy and labour, no matter how painless medicine had rendered the whole procedure. They preferred adoption of parentless children. But soon no orphans were left, except for the ones whose parents were victims of war or accident. It was in the late 23rd century that a limited "baby boom" occurred due to the economic growth of China and other Asian nations, only to die down again as soon as western morals caught up with them.

It was late in the 4th millennium and still man – and nations – craved for what they had not: on the one hand, federations and confederations were broken down into their members who clamoured for "national identity and independence". The only federal state still standing were the United States of America while the former European Union, after having

---

[15] It was originally signed as regarding the treatment of the wounded in war. In 1949 three more conventions were signed, regarding the humanitarian rights in armed conflicts, the second the treatment of P.o.W., and the third the protection of civilians during war.

expanded to Asia and Africa, had disintegrated into the nations that had originally formed it. On the other hand, smaller nations in Asia and Africa formed alliances, adopting the motto that "strength lies in numbers".

In 3815, the globe was ravaged by small time wars and several mini-states had emerged. The frontiers among them have been fluid, and largely determined by the flow of the surviving water bodies. Some of these states inherited the obsolete nuclear arsenal of the now defunct great coalitions of states – but none of their wisdom.

In this war for survival, all arguments were evoked; tribal, religious, national laws and principles served as pretexts for the domination over rivers and lakes. The industry of desalination of the sea water boomed for many years in the western countries, but the high cost made the purchase of this purified water by the poorer countries prohibitive. In May 31 of the year 3848, the government of the day of one of these precarious and temporary mini-states – later historians could not say for sure from which faction the guilty leader came, as in those days some governments counted only hours before they tumbled down while another contestant seized the power – in a nationalist and religious frenzy, sent its nuclear missiles to the rest of the world. It caught the whole planet unprepared; no strike-back took place. The lands that were not immediately obliterated were contaminated by radiation as the winds carried the killer cloud in all directions.

After the explosions, the icebergs at the poles melted down and the waters rushed in. Satellites kept feeding those manning the terminals in the spared lands with photos first of the holocaust and then of the modern cataclysm: The map of the world had changed beyond recognition. Gone were the continents. The three great oceans had merged into one, its waters sloshing around the islands that were formerly the peaks of the Rocky Mountains, the Sierra Madre, the Cordilleras of

Andes, the Pyrenees, the peaks of the Alps and the Himalayas. The world was now a single ocean, studded here and there by bigger or smaller islands. So many civilizations had been lost forever.

In some continents where high mountains had formed a protective ring around an extensive acreage of land, large wastelands could be seen, though they had been contaminated by the killer cloud.

Satellite photos showed that in these wastelands several populations managed to survive for some time. In the genes of these people radiation had wreaked havoc. Unable to restore their world to what it used to be, they roamed the land in gangs, and at the land's end they used every sea-going vessel that could be salvaged, retrieved or invented from the material that was at hand, pursuing a dreamland they called Utopia, which presumably was what was later called Safeland. Life for the survivors of the contaminated areas resembled the primitive nomadic life of the primeval men. They had adapted their organism to absorb nutrition from the radiation still clinging to the soil, the air and the waters. But as each generation, diminishing in numbers, brought more deformity and misery, they finally gave up and disappeared completely.

In Safeland, scientists and explorers did not dare enter the radiation stricken areas for obvious reasons. Many millennia passed and the waters had slightly receded before they ventured to fly over the devastation, and many more before they made up their minds to land, wherever the geology of the place made it possible. The wretched inhabitants were long dead. It was the relics found in the areas that gave substantial and supporting evidence to the testimonies of the photos provided by the satellites.

What was amazing was that some photos caught those people in the act of sex. Safelanders found out, to their dismay, that sex was among the top preoccupations, the only entertainment, of the "nuked" as they came to be called. No preoccupations for procreation were involved of course. No sentiments either. Sentiments were a luxury the "nuked" could not afford. Sex for them was simply the satisfaction of a bodily need, such as eating to the hungry.

To the spoilt eyes of the pre-nuked, nuked-sex had nothing to do with the act of love. Neither with rape, as the former suggests consent and the latter the lack of it. The women did not consider that they were taken against their will, quite the contrary, they were grateful that a functioning man had come their way. More stable alliances were formed, when two people liked each other and decided to stick it out together. However it did not mean exclusivity or monogamy, sex was like drinking water: where there was a fountain, one profited from it.

Safelanders would have been pleased to comment that it was sex that undid the nuked, had not their scientific knowledge showed them differently. As a matter of fact, it was the continuous intake of radiation and their adaptation to it that exterminated them. Yet, the same would have happened had they not adapted their organisms to radiation. Only their end would have been quicker. The nuked were in a "Heads you win, tails I lose" situation. Poetically speaking, one might say that their adaptation to radiation reduced them to radiation motes themselves, wandering aimlessly in the atmosphere, until time would unburden them of their radiation load and send them to non-existence for good. But there were no poets to be found among the Safelanders. Among the nuked neither.

Safeland is a masterpiece of a city. Actually it is not a city in the geographic sense of the word, rather in a political sense. True to a parody of the ancient Hellenic ideal of democracy, the city has its citizens and its humanoids. The status of the humanoids is similar to that of the ancient slaves. Safelanders consider themselves lucky, as they know that in other parts of the planet, entire coastal and island countries went under the waters, though the entire extent of the catastrophe has never been made known to the public.

Small communities are scattered across the land, all reporting to the High Council in the capital. In this part of the planet, the flora and very few of the fauna is left intact to flourish and to develop – not quite – unimpeded: their growth is checked by the appropriate authorities that watch over the balance among the species in the environment. Plants and animals are not supposed to develop at the expense of the human race. The numbers of each species are checked by the minute, so that no error will occur. Particularly the animals, useless now – women do not eat them, do not ride them, do not use their skin or their wool – will not be tolerated to eat up precious food. Most of the plants are also useless but they do not consume anything and they provide women with the basis of their food, so they have earned their daily meal ticket in Safeland.

Back in the year 3848, when the missiles eradicated the greater part of the world, Safeland was the only place totally unharmed. As people had been following the water courses for centuries, the demographic map of the world had been accordingly altered. As a result, the lucky population that survived at the time consisted of a mixture of races and nations. Later statistics from the census department counted half a million of Caucasians and two hundred thousand Africans who lived permanently there. When the survivors realised that they were the sole inheritors of the earth, impulsively, men and women alike, they thought of retaliation, so that the perpetrators would pay for their crime. But it was very difficult to determine the perpetrator state on the one hand, and on the other, it was easily assumed that the guilty party too had perished, either because of the radiation cloud, or under the waters. In the former case its inhabitants did not vaporise instantly, their demise must have been slow and painful. Many lived to see their beloved badly scorched, eaten away by cancer, while those who still could, would have attempted to escape from the killer cloud.

Politics at the time were still (literally) running with the tides. The old traditional bipolarity between the U.S. seen as the capitalist enemy of the people, of democracy and of self-determination of the nations and the Russians, thought of as a benevolent power, willing to lend a helping hand to the oppressed, was long abandoned. After the fall of China and as the 4th millennium dawned, there were no more super powers. Old enemies struck alliances, and neighbours who normally had been friends for centuries found themselves fighting over the river that separated them and at the same time had irrigated their fields and kept their herds from thirst. The ideologies of communism and capitalism that had so seriously divided the peoples of the earth were forgotten. Religious differences had also lost their reason for being. The urge for survival, more pressing than gods, kept people at each other's throats.

Safeland, being on the outer fringe of the mushroom that had hit most of the vital cities in the world, did not suffer any immediate damage. Only a coastal ribbon about half a kilometre wide had vanished under the sea. The day after brought reason and second thoughts to the survivors. The initial impulse to strike back collapsed. Their territory, protected from the west by gigantic and impregnable mountains, behind which the waves crashed with unrelenting fury and the poisonous clouds were dispersed or deflected, surrounded by sea from all the other points of the horizon, was the only inhabitable place left on the planet, as winds must certainly have carried radiation above the perpetrator state as well.

Immediately after the detonation, huge Aeolian fans were erected around the shores and the mountain ranges that framed Safeland, in order to keep the radiation cloud at bay. In these days, one could not trust one's fate (and survival) to the winds, no matter how favourable they might be. After all, the gods of the winds, in most theological systems, were male.

* * *

At this point Masculina buries her head in her hands. It was so cruel, yet the only viable solution. She recalls her country's modern history:

Each day, caravans of survivors arrived from neighbouring states, by sea, air or on foot over the mountains, carrying with them, apart from their precious belongings and handicapped beloved persons, molecules of radiation. Instantly the population was divided in two groups: The first demanded instant mobilization to help the refugees. The second?

At the time, men were already not counted as decision makers. Those who kept true to their sex were going from war to war, blind executive pieces in the checkerboard of the warmonger visionaries, while the rest who were at home were completely domesticated. Cloning was superbly developed – the days of Dolly the sheep were long forgotten – and women had created a whole army of androids, specially designed for mating; no words were needed, no feelings got in the way. Other clones were made for hard work, others for scientific research – no more guinea pigs (guinea humans or humanoids?). Humanoids and their mechanical assistants were never permitted to achieve the intellectual or the emotional level of the humans that would enable them to threaten their masters, as so naively writers of the previous millennia predicted in their science-fiction stories.

At the first influx of the foreigners, committees of relief were formed and sent to meet them, but no entry to the spared land was permitted. The first of the reception and relief committee members were instantly contaminated by radiation, while the refugee camps became a breeding ground for all sorts of infections and illnesses. The women inside convened a secret meeting where they decided to send some thousands of expendable androids, programmed to self-destruct at the accomplishment of their mission. Their mission was the extermination of all that breathed out there, be it man, woman, child, dog or horse.

The same assembly of the night of July 3, 3848 proclaimed the creation of Safeland, and put down the first article of its constitution that would later become the founding principle of its whole legal system – which was surprisingly simple: *"It is hereby proclaimed that a new state is created, sole inheritor of the human civilisation, after the nuclear destruction of May 31, 3848. It is hereby declared that safety for all its inhabitants will be the essential preoccupation of all its ministers and administrators. It is therefore announced that this new state will be called Safeland. Safety is guaranteed by this constitution."*

The second article was equally simplistic: *"Having witnessed all the destruction caused by the former world, we denounce all former geographical data as regards to the position of our state on the planet. It does not matter on which former continent or state Safeland lies. All geographical references will be omitted from the vocabulary of our country. From now on, the only state on the earth is Safeland."*

Safelanders did not find it difficult to comply with this constitutional imperative. Until a month ago they were part of a large world, which, in a matter of minutes, had diminished considerably and shrunk to a fraction of its former size. But now, the satellites showed that they were alone in this world, except for the unfortunate ones who had stayed behind on the radiation ravaged territories. There was no meaning in defining their position on the map in relation to other countries. There were no more other countries.

At the dawn of the following day, the army with the special mission departed. No sooner than two days later, a huge electro-magnetic dome was erected round the spared area, and has never come down since. Ever since, the blasted part of the world is known as the "Outside". No Outsider is permitted to enter Safeland – not that any has reached its outskirts after the cleansing operation.

It was to be expected that this vagueness about the coordinates of Safeland would be the cause for speculation as to its position on the globe. Every once in a while, a new theory would come up, placing the spared city now in America, now in the Russian steppes, in central Europe or in the former South Africa. In the 14th millennium, a historian claimed that he had solid evidence that it was the soil of the legendary Atlantis that held them all.

According to the findings of his team, the nuke-bang on the one hand and the flood that ensued on the other, released enormous forces in the core of the earth. As some continents settled down on the bottom of the sea, Atlantis was dislodged from its submarine nook and up she emerged, sparkling and glistening in the sun, salt water dripping from its mountain peaks and rushing out of her valleys and ravines. The ancestors of the Safelanders, the first inhabitants, were those who at the time of her emergence were close by, in ships, submarines or air-planes, fleeing their nuked countries, in the look-out for safety for them and for their families. It was also suggested that Atlantis was a vast area of the central Aegean seabed, probably the former Cycladic and Sporades island complex, with its west guarded by the peaks of mount Olympus and the rest of the mountains that extended farther to the west and north-west.

The females thought that the concept of Atlantis was dangerous to the peace and order of the land. The myths it evoked of civilizations transplanted from other galactic systems and of all-powerful gods constituted the most fearful elements of the past. Also Mount Olympus with its sexist gods and empty-headed goddesses, full of human passions and weaknesses would be like a plunge in the murky waters of a sinful past. It had better be forgotten. So, when the historian asked permission to shoot a film which would combine the ancient myths with his present findings, permission was denied. After the rejection of the Atlantis theory, scientists stopped all efforts to locate the identity of Safeland's former host. Besides, this activity was against the constitution of the year 3484, still valid after all these millennia.

Masculina's mind wanders back to the first days of her country: Safelanders soon forgot about the killer army they had sent to the Outside, after all they were only clones, nobody loves clones – actually nobody loves. In her struggle for justification for the decisions of her ancestors, she keeps on reasoning and arguing with herself: The travellers, they were condemned by their earlier exposure to radiation, sooner or later they would die, and, had they been allowed to penetrate into the clean territories, they would have taken the untouched ones to a cancerous death. And then no life would have remained on earth.

Women would not permit man's impulsiveness to destroy the human race. Because it did not matter who punched the button. What mattered was who had created those weapons, who had fanaticised their holders to unleash them, who, finally, did not keep a close watch on his arsenal. Woman had only one mission, to continue the human race. Man on the other hand, although assigned to help her with her task, was led astray by his lack of discipline and his penchant for violence. Women destroyed those who threatened the existence of mankind.

Man, because of his imperfections, did not have to be terminated; he did it himself. His longing to become and to act as a woman gave precedence to the X element in his structure; his male features gradually declined until utter effacement.

After the "nuke-bang", women consciously ostracise men. A special clone body is formed with the sole task to cleanse the sperm banks from the Y spermatozoa, so that women who opted for traditional child making would bear only girls. Only some specially selected Ys were saved, to produce male sperm in order to assure fresh sperm production for the banks. Needless to say that the clones used for lovemaking were programmed to be barren as no unchecked breeding was to be tolerated. The resurrection of the family pattern and other possessive behaviour would endanger the order in the land.

No men, no competition, no danger. Life was really safe and easy. And boring. After the 13th millennium the sperm banks were exhausted. So were women: Artificial insemination, although the ensuing pregnancy was entrusted to special incubators, was too much trouble.

Besides, women themselves were changed. Most of their female features had atrophied. First of all went the breasts. As breastfeeding had been abolished since time immemorial, and as pregnancies did not disturb the mother's body, breasts atrophied, until the first generation with no breasts appeared. The shape of the body changed, it became more slab-like; no waistline, no hips. Next the hair disappeared. As cold weather had entered the sphere of fairy-tales and beauty was not sought after as there were no men around and no competition among sister-women, hair became useless. No physical exercise resulted in a slackening of the skin. Female bodies start resembling a potato sack on two legs. The colour of the skin, because of the stable temperate climate and the same nutritional regime shared by all, gradually becomes uniformly white with an ochre tinge. Only height makes the difference between Safelanders now; there are the tall ones and the not so tall ones, and finally the short ones. The time to end all racial discrimination has truly come. All the earlier struggles had been in vain.

The rest of the changes were internal and came much later, long after Masculina and her friends had passed away. As the uterus stopped playing the part of the natural incubator, it shrank to nothingness. The vagina gradually filled up with tissue and the vulva was sort of eroded from the abdomen. The endocrinal system underwent a profound transformation, as female hormones were, generation after generation, mingled into one and then disappeared completely. Only a genetically moderated quantity of adrenalin remained, to stimulate women to carry on with their boring existence.

The brain was "upgraded" genetically with memory chips that supplanted the institution of education; the cortex, little by little, shed its numerous layers, because the chips did its job. Only the core of the brain was necessary, to sustain the indispensable functions of life. However, as life grew easier and increasingly prosaic, some millennia later the memory chip disappeared, as memories and knowledge were best forgotten. One might say that too much upgrading annihilated all progress.

The human race – women only – will then (in the year 296.561) be multiplied by pure parthenogenesis.

\* \* \*

Masculina was the last to have been born "traditional style" by a woman who chose to be inseminated by male sperm – which showed that its owner had been one among the last and fast declining men – just before this procreation technique was permanently abolished. Weak as the sperm of the donor was, it bequeathed his daughter the weak stubble that gives her face a faint masculine hue. It also endowed her with fragments of his collective male memory. In earlier times she would have been a man.

At the time she was born, humans, albeit only females, were still rational and their babies were given each a distinct name. The reason was purely the facilitation of the task of the administration in monitoring the numbers of the citizens. It was essential to know how many were to be fed and clothed, how many exited this world (died) and how many new arrivals were to be expected.

It was very difficult for the authorities to decide on the name to be given to the baby born on September 29 of the year 125.860 – the time of birth was not required as no two humans arrived on the same date and besides it was standard procedure that babies would be delivered at noon.

This particular infant deserved a male name as it still carried this gene Y, although it had not affected its appearance, but also a female one as the latter was the predominant element. Only later, in puberty, predicted the scientists, would some scant hairs grow on her face, something like the beard of the ancient and hateful men. But this was no concern for the present. So the name remained a difficult issue, as on the one hand it would be grotesque to call an apparent female with a male name, and on the other, male names were erased from the city rolls in these days, as no more men were around to claim them and to bear them meritoriously.

So they decided to call her with a female-sounding name but which denoted clearly the pattern of her chromosomes to the society. As with the previous males who had been in the same situation in the past years, the female pronoun was used in her case too. So little by little Masculina learned to answer to this name, and the others would cover their mouth with an open palm and snigger behind her back. The tell-tale name was chosen as a warning to the rest of the citizens that they should not get too close to this last Y. It would also help her to better be integrated in the all-female society. A purely male name might have given her the false idea that she was a man and thus led her to behave like one, with very unpleasant consequences for her and the whole society.

Her family could not hide their shame no matter how much they had wanted to because, after routine calculations and gene tracking, the birth control authorities were expecting the last male to arrive. It was decided that it would be left alone to live and expire peacefully when its time came, as females never practiced wilful murder if it could be avoided. But to be on the safe side, they neutered it, as surprises in this field could only be unpleasant.

As she grew up, she felt she was different. So did the other (female) children of the city. When the first signs of facial hair appeared – to the utter horror of the authorities the colour, purple, was an insult to the eyes of the public – she hastened to get rid of it. The only means available was the obsolete razor, as electrical depilation, photolysis or even the herbal ancient methods or waxing, had disappeared completely. On the one hand women had no more hair, on the other even if they had, they would not have busied themselves anymore with it. So at first Masculina shaved her cheeks. Later, some girls emitted signs of attraction towards her. When she realised that it was the weak latent man inside her that drew them to her, she left the purple hair on her face grow free, though an old fashioned fully grown beard it was not.

She will not live to see the absolute degeneration of the human race. It will take a very long time after her death to reach the parthenogenesis state. Women still multiply by using sperm from the special banks. For the time being, she ponders the fact that with her, all that relates to males will die. She is the last of a lost sex.

Felina puts down the book and sits across from her friend. "I want to show you something" she says. From a concealed pocket in her sack-like garment she produces a batch of photographs and sketches. "I got them from the Lecturer in Anatomy of the medical school of the University. Look how we used to be!"

Felina is also a student of the Old Medicine Faculty. As a scientific subject it is outdated, as diagnostic and therapeutic methods have changed, and as the human body has also changed. It is for historic reasons that she wants to know how her forefathers and foremothers were built. The prints she is showing to her friend do not depict men and women but human organs; to be exact, sexual organs. Their curiosity can not be satisfied with academic descriptions; on the contrary it is highly excited by the pictures they see in books and films, where people are dressed or posing as undressed. Except for the female breast that is liberally shown, all the rest are artfully hidden. Even in some pornographic films, things are a blur of bodies in motion, while the acts shown are incomprehensible to them, sometimes even outrageous and utterly disgusting. Scientific photos help.

The two friends start whispering and giggling, as if to avoid being overheard, and at the same time feeling that what they see are literally "private parts", not to be shown around carelessly and indiscreetly. Felina slightly reddens as her friend exclaims: "These are the organs for lovemaking. Penetration. It has a symbolic connotation of invasion. Come to think of it, it makes one think of destruction, if you consider that at their time there was a primal state of virginity in the life of women. No wonder ancient women loved it and at the same time loathed it. This is why ancient women loved men and at the same time wished to be rid of them! How I wish we were still like that! Imagine what you and I would do!" "Hey, don't say such things" says Felina, her blush slowly fading away. "I am sure I would never make you hate me", the other one goes on.

Felina's cheeks flare red again, as she secretly savours the scenes from a film that she has not shared with her friend, who, fortunately, seems lost in her own personal reveries. Felina feels a funny tickle in her lower belly and her breath comes in short, laboured puffs. She lies back in her chair and closes her eyes. As a precaution against hugging herself, she throws her hands away from her body, down the arms of the chair. At first, her mind is filled with a blur of bodies in motion, one light skinned, the other slightly darker and more muscular. Soon the image clears. A long-limbed woman, radiant as the sun, is lying on her back on a rug on the floor and on top of her a swarthy male is busy getting his hands and his mouth full of her. A tiny inky- black scorpion is tattooed on his left shoulder-blade, a darker, indistinguishable shadow among his lightless skin. Their soft moans gradually escalate to agonising groans, and Felina wonders if it is pleasure that is causing them or agony, or if pleasure and agony might have something in common. Once again her imagination sheds away the layers of ugliness and shapelessness, in her mind's eye she is now the old times woman with the auburn hair and the delicious curves, fully equipped to enjoy what the couple in the film seem to be enjoying. It is this image that she always assumes for herself in her imaginary travels and she knows that Masculina sees her in this way too. Now she takes the place of the unknown woman in the film, who is writhing under the caresses of the man. She is actually her. Now the stranger pulls away from her (Felina) and grabs a bowl of cherries from the side table standing nearby. The woman in the film seems to know what is to come and welcomes it with glee, but Felina is slightly scared, although she has witnessed this very scene quite often and she too knows what to expect. She trembles with expectation and excitement as he spreads her legs further apart and starts filling her pulsing emptiness with the shining fruit. Then he starts licking the contour of her breasts, then gently biting her nipples as he murmurs "let them there to take your flavour honey!" Felina is beyond herself with exquisite pleasure as his tongue goes down to her navel, then to her Venus mound and to the flesh beyond. Her insides are on fire, she feels faint with pleasure and then …frustration. Now she feels his teeth nibbling at the protruding cherry. He takes it to his mouth, he chews it and spits the pit away. His fingers retrieve the rest of them, one by one, and until every cherry is consumed, he remains sitting between her knees. While he eats, his member softens a little but as the woman starts heaving and thrashing and sobbing in her need, he becomes hard again and enters her. Their frantic rhythm is hard to follow, Felina disengages herself from the fantasy and becomes the distant observer, the voyeur, because unlike them, she is unable to find release from the sensations that weigh heavily upon her.

The film goes on to reveal that the cherry woman, as Felina likes to call her in her (few and) lonely wanderings, found the scorpion man and their love-making highly addictive and decided to drop the affair. He did not look her up either. As she explains to her mother on the phone, she cannot sacrifice her independence for the sake of a nice roll in the hay.

Embarrassment spares the mother from the spicy details. Then she went and had two cherries painted indelibly at the inside of her right thigh, an image she never explained to her subsequent lovers, no matter how pressing their questions. One disastrous marriage, a divorce and one ungrateful kid later and a lonely life ever after, she still never seeks out the scorpion man though now she regrets having lost him. Not that she knows that their affair would have endured successfully the wear and tear of time. But the independence she so much cherished was just an illusion, a tale of the women of her era that cost her much and gave back nothing in return.

The story dates back to the early third millennium, so it is very difficult for Felina to comprehend the reaction of the heroine and her sentimental state of mind. Or rather the total lack of it. To her own confusion she does not wish to add her friend's aggressive "*idée fixe*": "Imagine if I had Masculina here with me, saying how it could have been us, and what a pity it is and how she would love to do this to me, and how she would never had let me go, oh her obsession with what cannot be anymore is sometimes too much for me".

This film and others of similar nature are stashed away in Felina's cellar. Romance and soft porn to her are almost the same thing. In some of them, more than two people are involved. She is fascinated with the colour variety and the beauty of them that does not have to be guessed at as is the case with her fellow citizens. Men and women of the past, their bodies milky white, café au lait, chocolate, golden and midnight blue, some covered with elaborate body paint from head to toe, all shiny with sweat, mingle together, trying to persuade the spectators that they are truly enjoying what they are doing. But the woman of so distant a future cannot even start questioning the truth or fake of the play-acting. To her, obsessed in her quiet and unobtrusive way with the pleasures of the past, everything is what it seems. These films are her little secret, the only secret from her friends and from Masculina in particular, with whom she feels free to share anything scientific, but not much on the emotional side, Masculina who likes to put labels to everything.

* * *

The two friends simultaneously shake themselves free from their private ghosts of the past and rise, as it is time to greet their fellow students from the university who come visiting. All the Old times lovers adore Masculina's garden and they come to admire it almost on a daily basis. Besides the paved path that runs through the lawn, lies an enormous piston, with a large jagged hole on its side. It must have been retrieved from the engine of a huge ancient sea ship of the middle 21st century. Traces of rust have been preserved so that its ancient origin will not be lost to the viewer. It looks as if it had been hit by something bigger, but scientists cannot tell for sure. It could have been an iceberg, a reef, or another vehicle, or even an act of aggression. Around the piston, red poppies pop up every spring. In the ancient oral tradition, poppies symbolised the blood of the innocent. Psychologists of Masculina's time would say that the piston is a phallic symbol, and the whole scene has been purposefully arranged in this way in order to commemorate the innocent who have spilled their blood because of male aggressiveness, which, in its turn, has suffered a serious blow and has been put out of order.

Greetings are exchanged, and Masculina offers coffee and tea. These two brews are offered as a sign of adhering to the old ways. The friends are not thirsty nor caffeine or tannin addicted. This offering simply shows that it is one of the elements of the past that bind them together. Masculina is very proud of the tea setting she salvaged from the city's warehouse. The cups – all six of them with only four saucers – are made of bone china the colour of cream with a gold – now mostly faded – rim and decorated with pale blue roses and green-brown leaves. Four of them are badly chipped, the fifth is so flimsy with use it is translucent and – miracle of miracles – the sixth is as good as new.

As a matter of fact, their Old times ritual includes saying prayers – not that they believe in anything, science has been so clear, but they have seen the miracles that faith in previous generations has performed. They also drink tea or coffee during the day and wine or beer in the evening, eating crude spaghetti with tomato sauce as meat and fish and poultry have long ceased to be served on humans' tables. It is true that these culinary habits have badly shaken the members of the High Council. To them it is unthinkable that a woman should spend so much time preparing pasta in the old way and crushing tomatoes with garlic and fry them in oil to make a sauce and a pathetic dinner of it. "Let the fat kill them all! Let them get permanent indigestion" said the doctors. "Let the interesting taste torment their libidinal appetites" said the psychologists. "Let their disobedience be not imitated by other citizens" concluded the administrators.

Sometimes the women play music that had been recorded during several periods of the Old times. The funniest of them all are some black vinyl circles, on the surface of which music has been physically etched. Of course, the quality of the sound is lamentably poor. There are other musical records such as C.D.s and films. And pieces of paper bound together, with pentagrams and tiny signs with peculiar tails, called notes, on which the ancient people used actually to read, and also to write music. How strange! The variety of different kinds of music is also amazing: pop and classic, folk and operas, baroque and renaissance music, rock and Gregorian chants, ethnic and hip-hop. Some times the women want to dance to the music, or at least to sway to the rhythm. Yet, few manage to overcome the inhibitions of their era and the clumsiness of their bodies; dancing, music, literature and poetry are pointless for the rest of their society. But their most favourite pastime is to listen to stories from the past told by their leader, Masculina.

Her gift in storytelling lies in her collective male memory; she is better endowed to absorb the history of their ancestors, more capable to reconstruct it and to communicate it. "Come on Masculina, tell us of Romeo and Juliet, of the French Revolution, of Colombo and the discovery of America", they cry in their strange, toneless voices. Their language is a mixture of many languages in which the English is predominant. Of course, speech has been simplified or, as the administration likes to put it, refined. The barbarous consonants and the round, soft and mellow vowels lie in desuetude. Simple sounds suffice to convey the meaning of what citizens have to say. But this strange assortment of people has managed, with the help of their linguistic professor, to read and understand the ancient English of the books of the 3rd millennium. Only their accent remains flat and without inflections that might denote any feelings.

Masculina willingly tells of the perilous sea voyages that took months or even years, of the slaves who worked the oars while the overseer set the rhythm with his drum and his whip, of the battles fought on horseback and of the mythical Centaurs, half men and half horses. She tells them of gods and demi-gods, of great monarchs and young urchins. She tells them of people who died of love, of hunger, of the plague and later of Aids. The women marvel at the emotions that overwhelm these stories. They are so sorry that phrases like "I love you, I would die for you, I can't live without you, you're hurting me, don't ever leave me, how could you do this to me, I hate you, I will never forget that, I will never forgive you, please forgive me, I miss you" on the erotic and female aspect of earlier life and on a more heroic (male) level words like "all for one and one for all, death to the enemy, I will die for my country," will never be uttered again.

What the others most probably ignore, is that, along with these romantic phrases, the ancient people pronounced other words as well that expressed anger and contempt and adjectives that were meant to offend and to insult and to humiliate and to hurt. Curses and maledictions and four-letter-words were uttered every other minute. Masculina – as half male – can well understand the rage and the fury, and the time draws near when she will start to curse her ancestors for their fecklessness and their frivolity regarding the future of their race. But for the time being, she gets carried away with the gaiety of her friends, and she gathers her memories of the stories she knows, ready to do her best to please them.

As her voice drifts in the lemon blossoms-perfumed air, scenes from the remote past come vividly again into life. The women can almost smell the salty breeze, hear the canons firing away, the song of the Sirens and the croaking of the gulls.

Today they ask for the story of Helen of Troy. Masculina obliges them and leaves nothing out. She tells them of the contest among the goddesses and how Aphrodite tempted Paris, one of the sons of Priamus and prince of Troy, by offering him the most beautiful woman of the world, although she already belonged to Menelaus, king of Argos; how they eloped together to his father's palace. Of the reproach that all the regal family openly expressed for this unbecoming behaviour, and of the doom his sister Cassandra predicted for her beloved city and how she was confined to her rooms so that the people of Troy would not be influenced by her words. People did not like her prophecies anyhow. How Agamemnon, king of Mycenae of the house of the Atreides and brother of the insulted husband gathered all the kings of the Hellenic territory at the port of Aulis. She said of the sacrifice of his daughter Iphigenia, because goddess Artemis was angry with Agamemnon for having killed her sacred deer. How she finally pitied the young maid and as the knife descended on the tender neck, she gathered her in her arms and sent her to the land of Tauris, to become priestess in her temple, leaving a deer at the place of the sacrificial victim on the altar. How the ships finally arrived at their destination and how the siege lasted for ten long years, how the heroes from both camps quarrelled futilely among themselves and how they killed each other.

She feels compelled to emphasise particularly the anguish of king Priamus over his dead son's body that has been defiled by the Greek hero Achilles, when the latter, after killing the former in combat, hitched his remains behind his chariot and was dragging him for a whole day in front of the walls of Troy, so that all Trojans would see their prince reduced to an ignoble cadaver. She tells them how the king of Troy pleaded with the king of Myrmidons that the body be returned to him so he would be able to put him to rest according to their country's traditional rites and to the natural laws of their common gods.

She goes on to tell how the war seemed pointless, until Odysseus, king of Ithaca, had the Greek men build the Trojan horse and leave it on the deserted shores as a gift; how the gullible Trojans gathered the fake gift inside the walls together with the fighters that lay in ambush in its belly; the fall of the city that followed, and then the ravages, the ruins, the fires and the pillage. No one was spared. Then she told of the return of victorious Agamemnon, who carried Princess Cassandra as his personal slave in his ships, only to be murdered by his wife Clytemnestra and her lover Aigisthos as they trapped him with a fish net in his bath.

She would like to go on and recount the story of the murdered king's children, Electra and Orestes, how the son killed the regicides, how he was chased by the Erinnyes that brought remorse, how he found refuge in Apollo's temple, how the god chased the horrible creatures away saying that in his land, people were responsible for their acts, so guilt was redundant. But she is out of breath. And, anyway, she can see that her friends have already had enough of the myths of the old world.

In fact, the women have been holding their breath for a long time. The scene that will haunt them for the days to come is that of the fall of

Troy. After the usual comments and exclamations are exchanged, they put their cups down and rise silently. One of them whispers a hasty "thank you" – another pointless and forgotten phrase – and they take their leave in twos and threes. One of the last to leave turns her head back and asks of the waving Masculina that next time, would she care to tell them a part of "Count Montechristo", which is another of the women's favourites as love, treason, miracles and revenge fill the narrative. She smiles as she nods her ascent.

Night is falling. Felina too bids her goodbye and walks to the gate. Dusk engulfs her. Masculina picks up the cups and glasses and goes inside the house. She puts them in the special device that will sterilise them automatically and instantly and then goes to her writing table.

She settles down comfortably and prepares to start her end-of-term-paper. First, she enters the current date: Sunday, Mars 22, 125.897. Then she types the title:

# THE LAST WOMAN IN THE UNIVERSE
## *Year 125.897, Safeland*

It is a cloudy autumnal morning, back in the early 23<sup>rd</sup> century. Rain is hanging in the air, the damp earth gives off the characteristic smell of rotting leaves. If finally it rains, it will be a good opportunity to test the new "wet" robots, specially designed for humid weather. The engineers will check the insulation of their mechanism, and of course the traction. Who wants a bunch of machines slipping on the wet tarmac?

Men are still smarting from the fact that they came close to total extinction. It is the fault of the women, "these brainless, fickle creatures, who dreamt of conquering the world – our world".

"We do not need them. They are useless". These are some of the slogans exchanged among men. When they realised that the majority of their sex was being diverted to effeminacy and soon there would be no man left, they decided to put a stop to this.

For the first time in man's history, they did not pick up the guns. They had learned from the enemy that persuasion does it better. So those who were still men, soldiers and professional killers, started preaching to their fellow men. "Fellow-males", they would holler, "take off your skirts, throw down the frying pan, put the steam-cleaner away, this is women's work. By doing as they tell you to, you condemn your own sex to expire. Brothers, this is not fair. Remember, we are God's chosen creatures, His first creation, for us He sent His son to die. Do you defy your God for the sake of women?" How handy is religion! What a wonderful pretext, what a sound support it offers to all political aspirations!

At first, these words fell on deaf ears. Yet, it did not take more than a hundred years, for men to form large groups, with the proper military structure, who regained all the important positions on the planet. Soon, the women were left stunned at the unexpected reversal of things. Although females had domesticated males, they had not as yet had the time to get organised, to become professional rulers of their environment. Bad premonitions spread among the female population. Soon their fears came true as the High Commission declared that all women who wanted to live would have to become surgically neutered. Men would use cloning to multiply. Besides, sperm banks would be cleansed from XX cells, so should a man wish for a traditional child, the automatic progeny selector would feed into the molecular incubator a male. The final product would be a boy. For some centuries, cloning becomes the responsibility of the High Commission.

However, after long barren years, these radical measures were little by little attenuated, and some women were genetically programmed to be born and later grow into either prostitutes or domestic help. There came a time when women were regarded as "furniture" because they were considered as inanimate and useful in the same way as the tables, the chairs and the beds. But as emotions declined, as tenderness vanished in thin air, men could live with no sex at all. All their adrenalin found vent in their wars.

Women, they claimed, are either silly and petty, which is boring, or clever, which is extremely dangerous. We *can* do without the former, and *must* do without the latter.

At the time, a man's life was his wars. He had to be bellicose to wage war, and to have at his disposal his personal army in order to win it. Cloning helped manufacture armies of obedient soldiers. Soon another class joined the ranks of the battling androids: the mild and effeminate men who still kept popping up here and there every now and then, despite all genetic programming. They had no place in the restored man's world, there was no reliable post they were permitted to hold or that they could be trusted with. So they accepted their fate as punishment for their earlier folly, and as atonement, hoping for a better social status in the future, which of course would never come: They were sent to form the advance guard of the armies, the human ballast or cannon fodder, and thus, they were the first to fall, when battle began. They were expendable.

In the meanwhile, some hard-core men insisted on keeping a woman, for their personal pleasure. In most cases, the women went back to their natural role as homemakers, and created pretty love-nests for their men. These men fell once again under the spell of women; they left the side of their women only reluctantly, all they wanted was to live in peace with their mates for the rest of their lives.

"Mayday, mayday", shrieked High Commission officials: no more women to endanger our coherence, our existence. This is the end, no more experiments, no more leniency to the devious enemy and no more indulgence to the wayward men. The treacherous couples were separated, and those who resisted were executed.

Under utmost secrecy some female genetic material was kept in the underground vaults of the government building, for scientific and historic reasons. As a matter of fact, these vaults remained under lock and key for centuries.

Time passed, and man explored space. Space travel took man to other galaxies, planets were colonised, and space-craft was developed to perfection. Their engineers managed to neutralise the time effect of space travel, as time and space are two aspects of the same quality, which man separated, so that they would be easily comprehensible and manageable. The intricate relation between time and space is evident by the fact that distances (space) have been measured in light years (time).

On the contrary, men were not interested in time travel. Going back in time in order to correct something that had put them in danger was not worth the time and the energy it would take. Though in the past they came too close to annihilation as a sex, now they knew better that to jeopardise their status as masters of the universe. Besides, if they went back and inserted an alteration in the fabric of history, they were not sure of the long-term consequences. It would take time and precious manpower to calculate the endless possibilities. It would be better to let the past as it was. As for the future, there was no doubt, it belonged to them. There was no need to travel to and forth in time, everything was as it should be.

Men found that life without women was a never-ending fun ride. They decided that no nuclear war should threaten their happy existence. So they meticulously inventoried all the nuclear weapons that were lying around in silos on the planet – the loose nukes – loaded them to specific space vehicles and sent them away to distant galaxies, where they knew no life had ever, or would ever, exist. Thus earth was safely delivered from the greatest man-made danger. Meteors and other celestial bodies were permanently monitored and, should the need arise, deflected by special rockets. Life for humans was safe from all external factors, but not boring, as they kept happily fighting and killing each other.

Life for man had always come cheap, even in the earlier times, when all it took was a tiny droplet of his seed. Now, it costs nothing, it comes for free. As no human touch is necessary for the creation of another human, the word child has lost all its former meaning. There are no children for men. Only enemies, who fight over each other's throne – or should one say throat? Death to them all!

As men get killed in their wars, they do not live long, though their genes were perfect for longevity. They are fleeting specks of matter and spirit, leaving nothing in their wake. Only chiefs and leaders, who used others to do their dirty work for them, might die of old age in their beds. It was said that as death came near, they would murmur how pointless it all had been, how the innocents came to haunt them, how the blood they had spilled made their immaculately manicured hands feel sticky. Some asked for forgiveness, nobody knew from whom. "Old man's mumblings", their entourage would say and discard the incident as senility-induced. The result of these short lives was that men stopped giving names to the newborns, they did not even think of giving numbers. Men died, fresh men came, that was all that counted. Names and other sentimentalities belonged to the past.

Needless to add that all religions were abolished. First because they preached love and peace, or thought and reflection, thus diverting men from their true mission, secondly because man was now omnipotent, he did not need the crutches that gods offered.

Back on earth, an unpredicted situation cropped up. As boys were painlessly delivered from the incubators, they did not experience the primordial fight of the passage from the maternal uterus to the outer world. As a result, there arose a class of peaceful men, of "lesser men", who wanted to have nothing to do with blood spilling. "Bring women back" they shouted, "if only as furniture", the most moderate among them added. Others hung banners inviting their fellow men to "make peace not war" and publicly declared that "man needs a family". It takes no wild imagination to find out how they were subdued.

As the numbers of mild and gentle men increased, the tough guys got tired of being always on the lookout for trouble within the confines of their own planet, while space was out there, waiting to be explored and …exploited. They found a way to turn liabilities into assets: they prohibited all access to public records, and they obliged these "lesser" men to learn a menial task: with the help of robots, their workload was not so heavy; this is why they could not be assimilated to the ancient slaves. Some of them were put aside, and injected with a predetermined dose of chemically produced testosterone, specially designed to promote aggressiveness but not ingenuity, and certainly not sexual drive. In this way men mass-produced worthless opponents, in order to continue their bloody games, on earth and elsewhere in the universe. After all, these lesser men had found their rightful place in the community and a way to be useful to their brothers. Mass destruction multimedia helped them considerably to annihilate hostile populations.

Human robots were more reliable than the technological ones. The former were easily destructible, while the latter were not. Many a time had robots and other mechanical assistants achieved an intellectual, sometimes even an emotional level that brought a violent clash between them and their masters, with lots of casualties for the humans. Why would man risk creating beings that might overthrow him? Simply because man is inquisitive – and immature as a child – and once he has achieved a goal, he has not the prudence to stop there, he will go on and on, until his creation surpasses him. Then he will have no qualms to suppress it mercilessly.

The human robots had to work a standard 10-hour day with lots of long intervals. They were housed and generously fed by the state. They gradually forgot about life with women, they worked and were, if not happy, at least content with their lot. In a span of two hundred years, all riots had stopped. No one remembered women.

No one? This is not true. Who would be more obsessed with women but the guardian of the government subterranean vaults, where the only remaining female genetic material was kept! He spent his early youth in fantasising about women, about sex, about women again. As he approached maturity, he decided to stop daydreaming and to act.

He started spying on his other colleagues, in order to find out if they were men of hard principle or easily suggestible and unstable males. After a month, he had selected his targets: two younger men and one older than himself.

The next phase was delicate. He had to become friendly, but not too friendly. He should not make them suspicious of his motives. For almost a year he said hello, he shared his lunch with them, he asked what was wrong if one of them was in bad mood but did not persist. He did not wish them to feel cornered with too much amiability. Besides, in their time, no one was friendly, every man was at each other's throat. Simple and lesser men that they were, they gratefully accepted his friendship and were ready to return his interest.

The final step was the trickiest: Initiation. If he failed to persuade them, they would denounce him to the authorities. Very cautiously he started saying how happy he was without women, what a pest the creatures had been. His friends heard him, but they did not share his enthusiasm. "This is a good sign", he mused. "My new friends do not hate women. Now, let's sow the seed of hunger, and cultivate their desire". He started recalling stories of happy couples, happy families, happy men who shared their bed and their life with a woman. In no time at all, he had them burning with craving. Plan number one which he had called "Recruit" was happily over.

Plan number two was "Woman and planet candidates". He told them of his plan: they would take the genetic material from the vault, and disappear to a far away galactic system, the environment of which had to be friendly to human life. There they would reconstruct her, and live happily with her ever after. This latter part "live happily with her ever after" was entirely unrealistic, the weakest link in the chain of his plans, but he did not know it at the time.

They put their heads together to choose the right woman. She only had to be young and pretty, no more qualities would be required. As the three of the four had no special knowledge of the past and of the female celebrities that had shone temporarily on the firmament of history and as none of them had special knowledge of genetic engineering, they decided that it would be wiser to accept the genetic material as it was and not try to modulate it to their tastes, as in this case they would need the outside expertise of a specialist. This would be a fatal mistake, because they knew that they could not share their secret with any third party; they had better keep their secret to themselves.

Now is the time to devise names for our heroes, to help the story unfurl.

The guardian will be called, for convenience's sake, the Chief. His older colleague will be the Elder, the two youths will be Castor and Pollux, though not half-brothers as their ancient mythical name-sakes. They decided to give a name, a real, old-fashioned name, to their team: they called it "Eve".

As they could have no say in the choice of their woman, they started looking in the galactic charts to locate the planet that would be their host for the happy remainder of their lives. The planet that wins unanimous approbation rotates around its sun in a faraway galactic system, where no human colony exists up to the moment, and no special trade relations have been established with the inhabitants of the other planets of its solar system.

Planet $X\Psi\Omega$ is selected because despite the profusion of oxygen in its atmosphere and the existence of water on its surface, its relatively temperate climate and steady temperature, no signs of life have yet appeared. In their clandestine meetings, the four conspirators change the name of "their" planet to Eve. Imagination and inventiveness are not their strong point.

Next, they must present their official excuse to the authorities for the space voyage they will soon embark upon. Castor, as more acquainted with administration procedures, places a demand for a space-ship for a long-term voyage, on the grounds of a scientific experiment, whose purpose is the location and the mining of precious resources in remote solar systems. A disclaimer of the mining and excavation rights flashes in Castor's screen, he clicks "Signed", and lo and behold, permission is granted by the Space Travel Authority or STA. He has also entered the photos of his companions as his crew, and obtains permission for them as well. The experts at the STA evaluate the data furnished by Castor and decree that the space ship will be ready for take off in exactly 150 hours from the time the permission was notified to the interested party.

That night was a night for celebration for the members of Eve. "Beware, we don't have much time", the Chief cautioned them. He soon relaxed, as there was no alcohol to be had, so that nobody would get carried away. It was decided that their precious cargo – minuscule though it was – would not be removed from the public warehouse until –01:00 hours. "Most probably they will never find out about the missing material, as nobody goes down there but me, and as no forced-entry marks will be left, because I will use my official key-card. Only pray that the computer will still recognize the code, after all these years, and pray that no one will be alarmed to see the almost forgotten code reactivated. Anyway, it is a risk we must take".

Time seemed to fly and at the same time remain frozen. The excitement of the Eve members is difficult to hide, so they take pains not to meet with other guards and members of the staff. The 149th hour is approaching, and the Chief walks unhurriedly down the corridor to the elevators. As he waits, he checks his pockets for his key card. It is there.

He steps inside the cage and as it descends, he hides his hands in his pockets to steady them. Underground 10 flashes on the panel and the doors slide open. He walks to the safe door and as he inserts the card in the slot and punches out the code, a brilliant idea congeals in his mind. "Routine check before replacement" he says into the built-in microphone, as having been granted permission to leave, he will have to check his charges before his successor takes over. The door clicks open, and the Chief enters the chamber that holds his – their – treasure. For a moment he panics, "I won't find it" he says to himself. But there it is, in a niche in the far wall, where it has lain for centuries. His trembling hands close around the invaluable vial. To be on the safe side, he replaces it with another similar one, filled with a tiny quantity of wood shavings. It will take a close inspection to find out that the real thing is gone. Besides, he knows that the closed-circuit sensor system went broke some centuries ago, and no one bothered to have it fixed ever since.

He strolls to the exit, passes the threshold and closes the door behind him. He withdraws his card from the computer slot and hurries back to the elevator. He presses Underground 0 and ascends to his former work-station. He changes elevators and goes up to the ground floor. His friends are waiting there for him. "All is well", he utters calmly, "we may go".

The trip to the space base takes them but a few minutes. "You guys seem to be in no hurry at all" says the director of the base. "The ship was ready to leave without you". Pollux and the Elder feel obliged to smile – the one cordially, the other politely – at the stranger's sense of humor. "You know how it is, last minute check", says the Chief. "All aboard now", he went on. "Just a minute, who is the captain here", asks suspiciously the director, I have this guy's picture sent by Central" he went on, pointing to Castor. "Yes", he stammers, "I am the captain, but my colleague here", pointing to the Chief, "is our scientific chief." "All right, go on, countdown starts in 20 minutes sharp. Strap yourselves in and I'll come around to check that you've done it right. I'll come to tuck you in" he says and laughs with his humor.

There is no time to lose with petty wise cracks, they all mount the ladder and file in the space ship. The Chief flips on the controls and the banks of screens come alive. As they strap themselves in, impatience is almost tangible. The Chief is afraid that if he turns his head, he will see the vault security men rushing to the base, screaming not to let this craft take off. The others are afraid that anybody who cared to take a close look into their eyes would see the image of a woman, floating triumphantly and seductively. "Treason, high treason, take them, the women lovers" they would yell.

The minutes tick painfully away. At last, the base director enters, checks on their equipment and their instruments, waves a hand at them and barks "Countdown is imminent". He saunters outside as the huge door slides shut, while from the loudspeakers the numbers are heard as each one of them is peeled off, leaving in his place his smaller brother: ten, nine, eight, ....one, go!

"We are on our way", they all exclaimed, "no one can stop us now".

It was a long voyage, which in the past would have taken several earth decades, as the distance was many light-years. Now thanks to the special nuclear turbines and the spatial mathematics, it would take them less than six earth months. The first thing they asked of the Chief, was to see the magic vial. "Here it is, here comes my – our – woman", said he. The ship contained one molecular incubator as standard equipment – for experimental reasons: if and when the space travelers found some relics of life, they could use the incubator to revive them, just to see if they could be useful. If not, the process was reversed and the resurrected creature would return to its previous state of relic – which would be used for Eve. The idea that the reversal process might be necessary in case the woman they expected turned out to be an ugly and repugnant creature never entered their minds. They no longer were in need of a name for their team, after landing on planet Eve, they would be its sole inhabitants. They decided to name their woman Eve, in order not to waste time with name searching and possible disputes on the subject.

During the voyage they kept their exuberance at a low key, because they could not believe that they had made it so far. Besides, they were not sure that the cabin interior was not being monitored by the terrestrial station. Each one entertained his own preoccupations, but did not dare to share it with the others, lest he be called naïve, silly, coward or any other adjective. Yet, their unity and their dedication to the common cause were still intact.

Five months and ten days later, their craft was touching the soil of ΧΨΩ. It took them some days to adapt to their new environment: it was actually soil, water and wind; a terrible, howling wind. "We must find a way to terraform the planet" cried Castor, "we cannot live with our beloved in such barren and wind swept plains". However, there was little they could do, as they did not have either the "know-how" or the necessary equipment. All they knew was how to reconstruct Eve from the material they had brought along. They had read all there was to know about cloning from minimal genetic material. They were ready to perform their miracle.

The space ship was secured against the wind with steel cables and they turned it into their base. The female cells were placed in the molecular incubator, and a synthetic placenta took care of the nutritional needs of the tiny creature that was rapidly taking human – female – shape. As days turned into months, they could see through the transparent walls of the incubator little Eve, and check on her growth. Three months later, a healthy blond green-eyed lean girl left the warmth of the technical uterus to enter an equally technical world.

During these three long months, the men had equalized the temperature of the upper and lower strata of the atmosphere, putting an end to the previously uncontrollable wind. Their little girl was not to have her silken hair tousled by the rapacious caresses of the wind.

They had also built a large but simple house and transferred all the necessary equipment to the front room. The space-ship remained anchored a hundred meters away, an empty hull now, that might yet come handy should any emergency arise.

The men were prepared to wait for her maturity, they would not force themselves on her. For the moment, she would be treated like their little daughter. How ignorant they were, daughters do not usually fall in love with their father. Besides, women in love are normally monogamous, they choose the one who will catch their fancy. This fancy may not last for ever and she may sooner or later look for another mate. But it is not in her nature to be a shared woman. It was only due to circumstances of extreme poverty and perversion that a woman was reduced to such a state in the Old times.

Alas, men were unaware of these details. What burned them, as the girl grew to womanhood, was desire and envy. How stupid I have been, each of them thought, I cannot share her, I want her for me, only for me.

It is true that during the initial stages of their plans, they had thought to clone her, so each would have their own copy. They had turned it down as too dangerous, because when more than one female came together, a secret was not a secret any more. Besides women have always been devious, they might well outsmart the men and start a female colony on the planet. Or, worse, they might restore matriarchy, send the men to outer space, and who knows what else might befall them.

A woman is safer when she is alone.

The rapid maturity process was used with young Eve, so that the men would not have to wait for the natural time span that would be at least fifteen more earth years. Besides, men have always been impatient; since technology came to their assistance, men rarely left nature do her job, quite the opposite, they interfered radically with it, speeding things up as much as possible. Speed, as Milan Kundera remarks in his *"Slowness"*[16] is the surest way to forgetfulness. However, this is not exactly the case with our heroes; they only want to gain time. Time to enjoy life with their woman. If there is something they want to put behind them, it is their loveless years back on earth.

In the one year that actually took the new female to pass from childhood to womanhood, she had arranged things in her mind in the way of her ancestors; having descended from an upper middle class family, Eve could function mentally and sentimentally within the frame of the family. For her, the Chief was her father, the Elder her grandfather, and Castor and Pollux her brothers. In her young heart and innocent mind, her own personal Prince Charming was waiting for her somewhere in the universe. He would arrive in his silver-shining spacecraft, fall instantly in love with her, and take her with him, in wild explorations of the galaxies and of their bodies.

The men pampered her and she rejoiced in the attention. Her merest wish was an order for them. But in the last couple of weeks, she had noticed a change come over them. When they thought she was not looking they were staring at her, and when she turned to return the gaze, they hastily averted their face with a guilty expression in their eyes. Among themselves, things had also changed. Gone were the friendship, the trust, the companionship. Now every one kept to himself, avoiding the others. The ex fellow traveler, conspirator, friend, had become a rival, a hateful enemy who had to be eliminated.

---

[16] KUNDERA Milan, *Slowness*, Faber and Faber, London, 1996.

Insecurity kept gnawing at the Elder's conscience. He knew he was old, not particularly handsome, and that Eve thought of him as her grand daddy. He was afraid that he would have no chance with her, and violence offered no alternative. Should he consider the use of force, not only the girl would hate him forever, but the others would find the perfect excuse to put him to death. If he could not have her, was it right that the others would? He would have to do something about it. Maybe trap her in the incubator and engage reverse? Or should he think of something more radical, a punishment for her and her future lovers?

The Chief on the other hand, felt quite sure of himself. "I am not old, I am simply mature enough to know all about love, no doubt she will feel the same. I'm not ugly either, so she will choose me, as the others are too young and inexperienced, and the Elder is too old. I'll be the lucky one. Besides, it's me who conceived of this brilliant plan and brought her to life. The least she can do is show some gratitude". How conceited he was!

Castor was the romantic one. He had instantly fallen in love with the girl, he himself almost no more than a boy, and was dreaming that she would return his love. But he was not certain; as most young people of the past, he had hope to sustain him, but also doubt to make him uneasy and insecure, to keep him from stagnation and to push him to action. The others, he thought to himself, would see her obvious choice, would accept it and retreat peacefully and gracefully. They might even go on living together; he and Eve as a couple, the other three as the rest of the family. The old sentiments of solidarity and friendship would return after a while. Probably they might even try to resurrect some of the ancient traditional celebrations, what was it called, Christmas or something? How cozy they would all be!

Finally Pollux, the adventurous and ambitious, dreamt of a mutual affection, where he and Eve would quit the others and their HQs, and go explore the rest of the planet, or maybe take the space-craft and cruise the galaxy, why not! They would make a wondrous couple, they might even become the pirates of the galaxies; a life of glory and adventure lay ahead of them. They might contest the predominance of the High Commission on Earth, they could become the rulers of the universe.

The days dragged on, and the whole group became introvert, taciturn and on edge. Eve kept to herself too, as she sensed that things would change drastically and soon, but not for the better.

It was late autumn in ΧΨΩ, and a fire was burning outside the house. Each felt fate drawing them to the fire. They knew that it was now or never. Whatever the consequences, the whole situation had to end, one way or another.

As Eve emerges from the door, they each rise, enchanted by the sight of her and spell bound by the ancient magic of fire, and walk slowly to her. They form a circle whose periphery diminishes as they draw closer to the center, Eve and the fire being the center. Instant realization hits them hard: they all have the same ambitions and the same intentions. The fire sparkles evilly in their eyes, and the girl is motionless with fear. Not for long. The men start fighting. Fists fly, fingers curl, knees and feet bend and flex to support the fighters. The Chief goes slyly for his knife, while the Elder retires equally slyly from the melee. "Let them kill each other, then the woman will have no choice but me. The whole planet will be our love nest". He had forgotten, in the excitement of the moment, his treason. A couple of months ago, when he realized that there was no hope for him and Eve, after some doubt, he had decided that if he could not have her, nobody would. "We are in this together you bastards! For better or for worse!" he would cry silently to them, trying to justify what he was about to do. He had then sent a detailed report to the Clandestine Resurrection of forbidden species Office of the Ministry of State. Ephialtes would be a suitable name for him. It does not matter that his ancestor betrayed a military operation to the Persian enemy while

Ephialtes the Elder betrayed a secret of a private nature to the authorities of his country, treason is always treason, and traitors have always been terminated. By all standards he was doubly a traitor: to the laws of his country and to his fellow conspirators.

The monitors and radars and the sonar had been left untended for quite some time. Particularly since Eve approached maturity, no one had a mind to watch out for visitors, as none was expected. Too bad!

The magic moment when destiny will play out the drama of the surviving suitor is shattered by the super sonic boom of an airship touching down. Castor is down and wounded, Pollux and the Chief are fighting and the Elder is still in hiding. From the super fast "intergalactic mutiny suppression force" craft, a multitude of black uniforms spill out. In seconds, the conspirators were mowed down.

Not even young Eve was spared. The Elder was discovered as he tried to run away. A moment of hesitation arose when the officer in charge thought of sparing him in order to take him back to earth, where he would be duly tried and sentenced for high treason. "But if the fact that he had willingly notified the authorities counts in his favor and his sentence is attenuated, what if other humans make a martyr of him?" The decision was instantly taken, Ephialtes the Elder was summarily tried, sentenced and executed on the spot. The bodies were instantly vaporized, the space craft that had brought them all the way from Earth dismantled and stored in the intergalactic force's craft, the building that had housed their hopes, their dreams and their fears demolished. A huge fan started blowing the remains, scattering them in the air. The future space travelers would find no trace of the little drama that had taken place on the $X\Psi\Omega$.

Back to earth, one of the members of the "Intergalactic mutiny suppression force", as he was debriefed by the *ad hoc* committee, remarked that it had been the easiest mission in his career, "a piece of cake" as the traitors were totally unprepared for the assault, "because they were expecting a peaceful life with a woman", the president of the committee added with meaning.

Naturally, the whole incident was erased from archives and history records alike, for obvious security and posterity reasons. As for the happy officer who had enjoyed the easiest mission of his career, he too was erased, together with his whole team. The generations to come should in no way find out the shame of the present administration: that a bunch of lesser men had outsmarted them for the sake of a woman. Always the woman, that evolutional mistake, that useless and treacherous creature. Every trace of her existence must now be erased. Woman therefore was deleted from human history.

The unfortunate incident slipped into oblivion. Men kept colonizing the planets with an environment similar to that of the earth. Rival factions proliferated and killing only to be killed the next moment was routine. No more boredom, vive paranoia.

The lesser men were the first to fall, so there came a time when all telecommunications and transportation networks came down, as there were no more workers left to maintain them. All equipment gradually ceased functioning. All fancy weapons of mass destruction were rendered useless. Only men remained, fighting with their bare hands to kill. Whole astral colonies were decimated as revolution after revolution exhausted the populations. Man had protected himself from all natural calamities, only to destroy his fellow men and be destroyed by them undisturbed. When technology failed, it seemed that men, inexperienced that they were in primitive and "manual" combat would cease this senseless killing. But no, men were too weak to subsist without their precious technology; their survival without it was a matter of mere days.

In view of the situation, the upper members of the High Committee conceived a simple, yet extremely effective plan: if the production of "real" men had slowed down, there would be less rivals to fight, less contestants for the universal domination. Now killing was not the issue, only absolute, undiluted and undisputable power counted. Every officer imagined all his competitors dead, and him the sole ruler of the universe. The plan found a vast application among the fighting crowds, because everyone was busy killing those who were still alive, so there was no time to think of replenishing the human stock!

There came a morning when the sun of a solar system rose to shine on its planets strewn with corpses while a red haze enveloped them all. And then another sun, and another. All around the universe, there were desolate celestial bodies, shining on lifeless humans; life was no more.

* * *

It is well past midnight when Masculina decides to call it a day. She stops her imaginary voyage to this non-existent world of men. She feels exhausted; piecing the narrative together has not been easy for her. It feels as if it was she who fought to death, she who masterminded the Eve plan, she who exterminated the traitors. Her right wrist hurts, because she started with the classic key-board typing system, in honor of her much admired ancestors. Of course later she had to activate the mind-dictating program of her computer, but all the same, she feels tired. "Tomorrow", she thinks, "I'll have Felina read this over to see if she wants to change anything, and then we'll take it to the professor. Now, go to sleep" she tells herself. Her dreams are a dull, throbbing red, something like an open wound.

She wakes up with the first rays of the sun. She is in no mood for walking today, so she punches her destination on the map of her individual transporter, and in less than a second she is at Felina's. Her friend is up and offering a prayer of thanks. She is thankful for having Masculina in her life, for being allowed to share this life with her. Contrary to the common disbelief, Felina feels safe in believing in something supernatural, benign and comforting but most of all, she feels that she is not alone, that she has someone to talk to when her friend is not around. Of course she knows, it is all delusion and self-suggestion. Besides it would be better if the authorities never found out her innocent but so untoward faith.

Felina's place is devoid of all personal items, as are all the houses in Safeland. They are simple houses, not homes, nothing more than living quarters. Only utilitarian items such as a bed or a chair have a place in a Safelander's house. No decorations are necessary, no appliances, as the whole country is free from dirt and dust, germs and pests. The women just exist in their chambers, eat their food in the municipal restaurants and attend the meetings that the administration orders them to. Then they return home to sleep. Day after day after day, the same monotonous, dull, dreary existence.

She welcomes her friend and invites her to sit down beside her. She takes the roll of film Masculina hands her and slowly unrolls it. Silence engulfs the two women. As she reads, her eyes fill up with tears. "It is so sad, and so unfair" she cries. "Have you ever known a time in history when life has been fair?" Masculina chastises her. "Well, what do you say!" she asks impatiently. Felina wipes her eyes with the back of her hand and goes on to confess her unreserved approval. "It is fantastic" she exclaims, "Professor Femella will be thrilled with your essay". "It is our essay, not mine alone. You know, when I was thinking of Eve, it was you I had in mind". Poor Felina blushes again and is so embarrassed that she does not utter another word. At least for some time.

The two friends decide to walk to the university. As they come near, they perceive an administration vehicle parked in front of the professor's office. They both freeze. But they know that they have already been noticed, it will be useless to take flight. They look into each other's eyes - they must avoid all public demonstration of affection like touching or kissing - and step boldly into the office. Professor Femella has shrunk in her chair, while the figure of the administrator towers over her. She wears the insignia of a high ranking administration officer, two horizontal silver thunderbolts – the less the thunderbolts the higher the rank, actually very few officers bear the two silver wavy lines and only one the single one – and the classic telltale brown sack-garment. "Young ladies" she says pompously, "or should I say 'young lady and young man'", her tone changing to ironic. "We have been aware for sometime that you have been up to mischievous work. What is it this time, are you planning to bring men back, are you dealing in forbidden articles of the past?" she asks suspiciously. "No, madam, quite the opposite. Actually it is a fictitious report about the past and the future. Here, take a look yourself" says Masculina as she proffers the film.

The professor closes her eyes lest her terror shows. But Masculina keeps calm as the officer starts to read. When she puts the film down, she too closes her eyes. When she opens them she asks who the writer is. "It's me!" cry both Masculian and Felina at the same time, each wanting to save the other from any unpleasant consequence. The officer smiles sardonically, misinterpreting their haste as a wish to usurp all the glory, each one for her own sake, but immediately checks herself: "No expression of feelings, feelings are useless and so is irony". "I ought to congratulate you, young ladies, for being so ambitious. This is a masterpiece that must be published, so that all our sisters will get an insight in what men have been. Even those among us who still harbor a soft spot for them, will be finally persuaded to do away with such notions. I am sure that there is no objection," she concludes as her gaze sweeps both students and their professor. She bids them farewell and hurries to her vehicle, the film in her pocket.

The trio left behind is badly shaken but Masculina is the first to recover. "That was close" she exclaims. And she goes on to explain that a misunderstanding – or rather a misinterpretation of her motives in writing this paper – might very easily have put all three of them in a very difficult situation with the authorities. "Now that this danger has been averted, all we have to do is sit back and wait". She knows that the administration does not lie, because there is no need to. The administration does not ask, it simply imposes its decisions. So if the officer said that her story shall be published, so it shall be. There is no danger that her superior may have a different point of view. All administration members have the same program installed in their brains, so their decisions are always uniform and unanimous.

Besides, space travel, on which the fictional work is based, had thrived in the female world, so long as there were still men around to man the ships and take them up. When men with the necessary guts and ambition and determination vanished, space travel came to a definite halt. The members of the High Council had ruled that it would be better to contain their lives within the limits of Safeland, as space voyagers might become too independent, and as a result too difficult to handle. When you could foresee a danger, there was no sense in going on and daring it; you had better nip all possibilities of unrest in the bud. But space travel was a historical fact that the administration did not care to deny as dangerous, so Masculina's story was well founded, and quite compatible with the history of the land.

Time travel was another story. It had always been absolutely forbidden under penalty of permanent exile to the past. If women were allowed to travel to and fro in time, if they had access to the Old World, they might do something that would change the course of history. One miscalculated movement, and the world might come crashing down on their heads. Imagine finding their community back to a man-ruled world! Such mistakes would not be allowed to happen.

Besides, if women were allowed to go back to the past, and then allowed to return to the present, they might well bring back notions of retrograding, of reinserting men in their lives, of putting up families. But as men are stronger and more violent than women, they would once again overrun the existing regime, and no one wanted to go back to the barbarous morals of the male world.

What escaped the perception of the enlightened administration was that this measure was not necessarily a penalty: if women could travel back in time, one by one, to find lovers and husbands, once they had found them, most probably they would want to stay there for ever, to the horror of the poor man. They would want to stay with him and love him and at the same time change his erroneous ways, indicate to him how this or that should be done and transform him – with their love – into an obedient husband. Only few of the time travellers, appalled by the primitive technology of those times, would want to return to their own era, but nobody knows what they would bring back with them: from long vanished viruses, to long lost sentiments. Too dangerous!

Tomorrow is the day that the paper written by the two friends will become public. The names of the two authors figure on the first frame/page along with that of their professor under the direction of whom it was written. Though it could have been inscribed in a mind wave and transmitted to each inhabitant of Safeland in seconds, the authorities thought it would be better to print it in film rolls.

As in all totalitarian systems of the past, the active participation of the citizens was indispensable. Everybody would have to act willingly, to move; each would have to get up to go to the closest distribution centre and ask for her own copy and read it. In this way all women would show that they acted on their own initiative. All women would – voluntarily – see how evil men had been, and they would consider themselves lucky to have rid their lives from such violence and madness. No one would consider that the authors might have exaggerated slightly, either knowingly or unknowingly, as their work was pure fantasy without any solid facts to lend the story some plausibility.

* * *

# THE LAST MAN GOES OUT
## Year 125.897, Safeland

Life went on, and the studies at the Old Times University came to an end. Most of the classmates, except for the "inseparable two", drifted apart. They sunk back to the dull life of a world without men, without memories, without the beautiful stories that Masculina used to tell to her fellow students. Professor Femella had to give up her post as some decades later the university ran out of fresh students.

Her last course on "Discriminations in the male world" had earned her a high position with the administration, as her spirit was "compatible with the principles of the nation". Her entire academic record was favorable to such a turn of things. The members of the High Council admired her because, although her studies had been a long dive in the murky waters of the world of men, she had come up clean, free of all contamination. And her students had been a credit to her, particularly Masculina with her convenient story.

"Remember my friends," she had said to her students on that last evening that had completed their circle of knowledge and their travel into the past, "every difference you observe in nature, is the result of different living conditions. Take the example of the human race. At first there was one sex, then its survival imposed a second sex, and now that survival is not threatened any more, nature has returned to the simple pattern of a single sex. Take the example of colour or racial discriminations, which has been the source of so many wars and theoretical debates in the distant past. Why were men born black and white? Because they simply lived in different climate zones. Those who inhabited the tropics had to have some kind of protection against the fierce sun. So their organism provided them with a higher dose of melanine, which in its turn blackened the skin, making it invulnerable to the sun. On the contrary, those who lived in the temperate zones did not need so much melanine, and this is why they were white. Finally, those who lived in the north, where the sun was rare, they had minimal doses of melanine in their organism, otherwise the beneficial solar radiation would not reach them. Now, at our time and age, where our climate is friendly, we are all white. The slight variations of red and yellow skin have been ascribed to the nutritional regime of each people. It has nothing to do with inferiority and superiority. Remember my friends, our environment and we are inseparable, we adapt ourselves to it, we become part of it. It is different environments that bring about differences, so do not let yourselves ever make the same mistake as our forefathers."

The applause from the amphitheatre caused some ripples on the still waters of the *intelligentia,* and ensured her entry into the government echelons (three stripes). Professor Femella belonged to the past, together with the rest of the class. Now the job description of the post assigned to her as "new morals engineer", ran like this: *(she is) responsible for the development of new morals in the interest of the safety of the people of Safeland.* It is true she did not have much to do, so she kept reminiscing about the University of Old Times and her students. She found it hard to forget the spirit of Masculina, her quest for the truth and the myth, her grasp of a reality that was long past.

Of her former students, only Masculina and Felina remained faithful to each other and to their shared values of the Old times. They kept on searching in their books or in those they borrowed from the library, and they enjoyed imagining the old days. Some evenings they would sip some wine and listen to the music, another they would take out a deck of cards and try to fathom what the ancients did with them. Very often the roles would be reversed and Masculina would ask her friend to tell her a story from the old world. Her motives were not very noble; in keeping Felina busy with trying to recount a certain story, she found time to think, undisturbed by her friend's wish to communicate. At such times she would wonder if the ancient men were wiser than she gave them credit for, when they would find many distractions to keep them away from home, away from an ever-chatting wife.

Some time after her 35th year, Felina had to contribute one of her eggs for the reproduction of the race as stipulated by the law. As a matter of fact, each woman at the prescribed age would have the biologists select her best *ovum*. Then the good doctors would extract it, and by the procedure of the automatic cell division would produce one pure girl, only XX. After incubation, the baby passed completely into the care of the state. In this way all girls came out the same, no deviations from the type-model, as if they were all molded out of the same cast. No rivalries came to stir them to action or reaction. Rarely would the administration demand some sort of action, usually in the form of actual participation in a project, such as the case of Masculina's imaginary work, whose sole purpose was the condemnation of the male world.

After meticulous consultation with the scientists and the researchers, the administration decreed that the birth quota would be one birth for every death. As the quantities of the nutritious elements available had been predetermined since the dawn of Safeland, when some kind of men were still around, and as it was rather risky to try to moderate the programming inherent in the crops – instead of raising production they might well destroy it – it was considered safer to control births – this was not difficult. In other words, if they could not adjust the food to their needs, they adjusted their numbers and therefore their needs to the food that could be had.

Besides, there was no purpose in regenerating the human race in large numbers if some of them would be condemned to suffer from malnutrition or hunger, as it happened in the Old times. Reproduction is the purpose of nature, but the production of malnutrition victims was something that the women, rational creatures that they still were, would not allow.

Felina felt no pangs of remorse for the egg she gave away to the community, no feelings of separation troubled her. The ancient concept of a bond between mother and child, of the maternal instinct, could not be applied in the case of woman and egg. The only human being she cared about was Masculina.

Two urges had been haunting Masculina since puberty: in the first place, she felt a longing, as if she had experienced the sensation in an earlier life, to be held, or contained, in a hot and snug place, which would be hers and hers only. It took her some reading to find out that it was her dormant male sexuality that tormented her. Her body offered no vent, no release.

The second ghost, bequeathed by millions of males before her, was violence. And if wanting to make love to a woman was a shame in her time, wanting to hurt someone was a capital crime. Sometimes when Felina could not understand instantly what they were talking about, or in a playful mood without a good excuse, all she wanted to do was grab her by the ...hair – it was not possible, women in the late 1255th century had no hair – the ears then – no, it expressed hatred and it was humiliating – then by the front of her garment and shake some sense into her! At times she would fantasize that she was bashing skulls, or that she was waging a – her – sword killing the enemy by the hundreds. Another fancy of hers, was that she was putting a whole village to the torch, trapping with her men those who tried to escape their horrible fate, then throwing herself on the women ... and the children. In these visions or nightmares, as the psychiatrist would have labelled them had she known about them, she was always a man, a male, a he.

She guarded her secret from all her fellow-students, and particularly from Felina. The idea of terrifying her best – and very dear – friend filled her with shame. And a good job she did, till the end.

Yet as the years went by, in the nights when she was alone, a mighty wrath toward her male ancestors overtook her. She would stand in front of her mirror and cry in despair: "Traitors, traitors to your sex, traitors to humanity. Nature or god or your parents or whoever made you men. But no! You had to become women! You have been so stupid, so frivolous. First you were the tough overlords, then you got tired and scared and let women take over. You did not resist the impulse to become like them. Look at me now! What am I? Supposedly an androgynous creature, but in truth I'm not even that. Half a woman and nothing of a man, that's what I am. That's what I've been reduced to. Look at the women of my era! Once upon a time they were mighty in their weakness, they could twirl you around their little finger, now they are hairless, breastless, shapeless, witless; now you wouldn't even spit on them. Soon their other female organs will go, what will remain of humanity? Nothing I tell you, nothing! Do you know, I am the last man on earth, this shadow of a man that I am. The only sign of my maleness is this pathetic stubble. Traitors, traitors, damn you! I could be a real man, and father children and live to see them grow up. All is lost, because of you, my forefathers, with your wars and your unconditional surrender."

Her lamentations varied only in form, but the essence was always the same: first wrath, then despair, then regrets for what could not be anymore. Compared to her fellow citizens who felt nothing, Masculina had a heavy emotional load to carry – and to hide.

As the years drew on, she came to hate all the symbols of the past that decorated her walls and her gardens. "How innocent I have been" she would reproach herself, "how gullible. I wanted to honor the memory of those who destroyed life for me and for all of us. Not only men, but women too, have been unreliable and irresponsible regarding the future. They deserve no honors, no respect whatsoever. Really, coffee and tea, books and traditions, all for nothing! It has been a trap, a clever trap, which I myself set up. I longed for the past, while the present has been ticking away. Things will go from bad to worse, as 'evolution' will strip women of all human and female characteristics. They will turn into amoebae, what a waste. And there is nothing I can do to change or to reverse things."

Soon she gave up her spaghetti evenings with her friend, and reverted to the tablets the state provided them with in the municipal restaurants. All the ritualistic customs she had held so dear were also given up. She stopped playing the music that had been a source for happiness for her friends of the years in the University and herself. No more card games, wine evenings and teas in the afternoons. Most of all, no more stories from the past! Enough was enough!

It was during one of those nights that she silently collected all the ancient machinery from her room and took down all the posters and photos. She placed them in a container and sent them back to the library and the archives warehouse first thing in the morning. When she came visiting, Felina was taken aback with the stark walls and bookshelves. "It looks naked", she complained, but she left it at that. She knew that when and if her friend wanted to, she would explain everything. But she would not be rushed.

After the impotent rage and the regrets, came reflection. She started to form in her mind a schedule that would have preserved the previous regime intact, for ever. At first she wondered if she should go back to the warehouse to retrieve some writing or recording material, but no, she said, better keep my thoughts – useless and purposeless that they are – in my head. No humans of the future will be interested in them. Only Felina may listen to them, but only out of devotion to me, not that she would really care. Better not take advantage of her emotions.

What ancient people lacked, said she to herself, was education. Not specialization, there was enough of this: so many sciences, arts and professions. And yet, at the time when society turned first asexual and then matriarchal, so many people were unemployed. This meant that they had not enough money to buy what they needed, but it also meant that they had so much free time at their disposal – as is the case with me at present, she noted parenthetically. These ancient people did not know what to do with all that time. But inactivity breeds evil. So, they started headfirst on the easy way to hell. Hell? No, such an old fashioned word, better say extinction, it is more exact.

Special "life lessons" would have been the answer. Our ancestors spent their lives studying sciences and statistics and foreign languages, but never did they study the facts of life. No one taught them anything about human relations or about human feelings. What is more, they should have found a way to pass their wisdom on to their children, in other words, they should have become first students and then teachers themselves. In order to achieve this, there should have been special schools, starting as early as possible.

On a first level, children should become aware of their rights. They should learn what their rights are and they should be taught to respect and defend them. Then they should learn that rights go together with obligations, and they should learn to honor those as well.

Every step of their life should be preceded by the appropriate corresponding lesson. First test, the sanctuary – though not always so – of the family, where some elementary rules had to be taught and upheld. Leaving the family behind and going to school, where a multitude of new persons enter the child's world, and new data keep coming in all the time is a new test, where again the child must adapt to the new environment.

The arrival of a new sibling is the first treason a first born has to come to terms with: where he was the centre of his world, the sole recipient of his parents' love and affection, now he had to share them and pretend – for the parents' sake – that he welcomes the impostor, the result of their treacherous actions. Some guidance on sharing would come in handy. Entering the university, or deciding not to, joining the army, exercising a profession, sexual relations, marriage, parenthood, separation, divorce, death of a beloved person. There were so many phases in a man's or a woman's life, so many decisions to be made, and he or she entered each phase completely unprepared. The positive or negative outcome was mainly a matter of chance, and secondly a question of perception, comprehension and clairvoyance, to say nothing of preparation.

In other words, people trusted their lives to the circumstances; this is why they invented destiny, kismet, fate, and one or more god or gods, benevolent or malevolent to justify the results. More often than not it was the malevolent one who came in handy, who took the blame for all the calamities that befell a poor – and irresponsible – human. No wonder that the world has come to this!

She wants to insist on the subject of education on the facts of life, to elaborate with whole diagrams and age charts and related matters as they form in her mind, but she soon sees the futility of the project – as it would have been called in the past – and – reluctantly – lets it go.

After this abandoned – because not viable – project, a sentiment of peace seems to overcome her. She has finally come to accept her situation, (she would not use the word "fate") as well as the situation of the world of Safeland. She grows passive as reconciliation claims her, at least to the eyes of the administrators who are charged with her observation. But in truth, deep inside her, it is a feeling of doom that has put paid to all mental activity, to all her aspirations and hopes.

Little by little she feels her strength seeping away from her, she senses the end approaching. And she realizes that another item has to be added to her list of "life lessons": the reconciliation with death. In her readings of the ancient literature she has often come across the fear of the humans for death, for the unknown that lies beyond and for the ensuing uncertainty. Humans should learn that although sad and disagreeable, old age and death are inevitable. Maybe, says she to herself, for the first time in her life caught in spiritual wanderings, death is an end but at the same a beginning of ...something else, of an existence in another plane.

Men and women of the earlier years, ignorant of such preoccupations, would dye their hair and have successive face and body lifts, just to keep old age at bay. How grotesque they looked in the pictures she has seen, with their frozen smiles and their marble textured skin. And the men, how pathetic with their hair dyed in youthful colours. Only the deeply religious persons who believed in their God seemed to welcome death as willed by Him, and as a means to a swifter reunion with Him. And of course those who were in pain or who found no joy in the future. Imagine, thinks Masculina, people often committed suicide because they had either been let down by their beloved or seen their fortune lost and their reputation destroyed. If only someone had been there to persuade them that, in due time, they would certainly die. But until then, they should go on with their lives, as time, the omnipotent healer, would alleviate and eventually take the pain away. Given time, they would smile once again.

* * *

As predicted by the scientists at the time of her birth, this abundance of thoughts and emotions combined with her memories soon drove Masculina to the road to natural recycling. No pain, no illnesses came to claim her from the land of the living. Only a growing helplessness made her spend most of the day in a chair, and later in bed. Her friend was terrified. She realized that the time for the permanent separation was near. She suddenly found out that she could not face life alone. Or rather she did not want to. But not wanting to aggravate her friend's precarious health, she did not let her feelings show, for the first time in their shared life.

As the days dragged on, Masculina gradually lost touch with her environment, it was clear that she could not communicate. In those moments, Felina's memory would drift back, in the happy years they had had together. She recalled though some instances when her friend puzzled her: it was when Masculina's gaze got fixed on her, and her mind was evidently wandering. Felina never learned where. At other times, her friend's eyes would glaze over, then they would close, and it would take some minutes before she would come back again. Despite her questions as to what she had been seeing and where she had been roving, the answers she got were always vague and evading.

Felina did not let these fleeting moments destroy the perfect relationship that bound the two women. In the final analysis, everyone was permitted to have some time to themselves, everyone was entitled to some private moments. It did not make any difference that Felina had never wanted to be anywhere else but only where she could be with Masculina. Except, of course, for her little lonely escapades with her films and tapes and DVD's about sex. The truth is, it was years since she had last threaded any in her projector. "Now is the time to send them back to the store house" she thought to herself. "Or, maybe I will not send them back, what for, who is there to see them and why? Better bury them in the garden and let them rot away. They did not do me any good, neither to any of us".

When the end came, it was peaceful and irrevocable. The lifeless body of her friend was handed over to the authorities for accelerated recycling, as was the custom. Felina was devastated. For the first time she really understood the deeply rooted need of humans for solace. She wanted someone more powerful than her to comfort her and to assure her that everything would be all right, that Masculina had not perished, that her spirit – or soul as they had called it – would hover above the universe, and wait to be reunited with her, in another world, where everyone would be as nature, or god, had intended them to be.

Now more than ever before in her life she chose to believe in the voice of her heart and not in that of the logic imposed by the scholars of her country. For the first time she let herself be carried away with what was expressly prohibited: faith in some sort of god.

Now that a couple of months had passed, her desperate need to believe in a superior regulator had somehow abated. So did her wish to be in the company of her fellow citizens. She retreated in Masculina's house quite often, as she wanted to take care of the flowers and the trees still left in the garden there. She preferred seclusion, away from the mass of the other women. She had always found them silly and petty, now she could not stand the sight of them or the sound of their voices.

She neglected her meals. She sent away the neighbors who came knocking on her door, alarmed by her behavior. She died in her sleep less than a year after the loss of her friend. The community was awe stricken; "How could she die so young, she had at least another 50 solid years ahead of her," they said. The coroner put her death down to "unknown causes", a very rare occurrence at the time. One of the members of the former intellectual elite of the days at the Old Times university mumbled that "she probably missed the departed so much" and instantly looked around to see if she had been overheard. Fortunately no one had been heeding.

Only with Felina's passing away, were the authorities entirely relieved of any fear of the old male element being reborn amidst them. As long as she had lived, she was the last link to the last Y, they had been quite fond of each other and she had been grieving when death separated them. She set a bad example to the other females. Or rather they, the couple, had been a bad example for their deprived fellow citizens. Thankfully, the principles on which Safeland had been built proved to be sound, as no trouble emerged among the other women, no signs of retrograde tendencies. The High Council was extremely proud of the tolerance it showed to the last sample of the past, and of how harmless it turned out to be. Hallelujah, the women had been convinced that they did not need the old male, they had been completely healed from their need for him; the world would be absolutely safe from now on!

\* \* \*

Life went on in Safeland, and evolution constantly adapted humans to their needs as they arose. A few millennia later, humans – women – were deprived of reason – as earlier they had lost their female characteristics – because they did not need it any more. Their life was safe from all danger, no challenges were left to make necessary for them to think.

But let us not forget that nature has one single purpose: the reproduction of the species. The women of Safeland who had managed to prolong their life expectancy up to approximately 200 years and reproduce only once in their life time, were against nature, they were useless. So gradually their life span was cut down to mere weeks, and during their short existence they reproduced constantly. Nature had taken life back to the amoebae. Life had come full circle.

As each generation brought forth simpler women, incapable of the simplest tasks, the old electro magnetic wall that had protected Safeland since the time of the nuke bang came down. In the thousands of years that had elapsed since, radiation had worn itself away from the Outside. The planet was once again clean and pure, almost virginal. The ozone layer had healed and the rays of the sun became once again beneficial to nature. Little by little the waters evaporated and large areas bared themselves to the sun, the rain and the wind. Hesitant at first, tiny traces of life appeared in the mud. As the elements were propitious, the traces became creatures, and nature once again improvised; wings, tails, scales, talons, beacons, nails, all came together to create life. Soon the inhabitants of Safeland, oblivious to the past and unconscious to the present dangers were discovered by this new all-devouring life. They were the easiest pray the new creatures had ever had. It took only a couple of days to erase completely every last vestige of the human race.

# CURTAIN?

It does not make any difference which sex we think is better, stronger, chosen by god or more worthy. If humanity opts for one sex only, the curtain will fall on a world without life. It is like condemning a world that has been born with two legs, to walk on one. The natural balance is destroyed as women and men are complimentary, indispensable the one to the other.

The scenarios do not stop here. People from all professions and vocations have their own explication on why this world will soon expire. Scientists say that our planet is already middle aged, some time it will have to die. The ecologists claim that the rise in temperature caused by the ozone hole over the North Pole, caused by the rise in carbon-hydrates in the atmosphere, will bring about another fatal deluge and most coastal countries and islands will be submerged. Futurologists warn about epidemics, and Christians all over the world are waiting for judgment day. Finally, catastrophologists of all sorts are afraid of a nuclear strike that will wipe out all life from the planet or a collision with a comet will finish the job that man started.

In the meanwhile, men and women keep fighting for pre-eminence over each other.

Thinking about the primal matriarchal societies, it is only a steady and peaceful existence we may imagine. Developments might have been slower. Metaphysical phenomena such as telepathy and telekinesis might have substituted the need for technology. But, just to be fair, inconceivable atrocities might have been perpetrated in the name of the community or nature, for instance preventive euthanasia to the defective new-born. This was the case of the ancient Spartans whose society was ruled by men. They threw the handicapped babies to the Kaiadas canyon. This might be a relic from the earlier matriarchal times. Whatever the practices of these primeval times might be, the fact is that sooner or later, man the dynamic would inevitably take the place he thought was his due.

Back to the present, and hopefully to the future! One-parent families are already in fashion the world over. In the past it was divorce, death or abandonment that left the remaining parent to take care single-handed of the children. Not in our days. It is choice that makes men and women wish for a child without the trouble of a permanent partner.

The children that are raised by one of their parents, most probably will carry on the tradition, and men and women will grow entirely estranged. Even in the remote possibility that some of these children would desire to raise a traditional family, they would not know how to live together any more. Who will grow strong and win and take it all, who will grow weak and surrender first?

This should not be the point.

The fact is that man and woman are complimentary, that life needs them both. They are not enemies, nor rivals. They are partners and as such, they are simply different, as nature has assigned each of them a different role in the common task of the reproduction of the human race. The man sows, the woman carries the seed, nurtures it and brings it forth. Should one of the sexes eliminate the other, it will be either boredom – in the case of women – or madness – in the case of men – and in either case, the end will be the same: no more human race.

The activities of human beings today do not stop at the reproduction of the race. Today a person is what it really feels, and not what nature, evolution, society and law dictate. A person is aggressive or passive, an athlete or a scholar, introvert or sociable, away from labels and classification pigeonholes. Contrary to common belief, a couple is happy only when the man and woman are different from each other, when the one compliments the failings of the other. If they are identical, first they are incomplete as a unit as both lack certain elements, and second, inevitably they will become rivals.

A couple is a complete circle; nothing is missing, and it does not fit with other shapes or even other circles. It is also the reflection of the theory of duality: god and devil, immortal and mortal, man and woman, good and evil, all separate beings that form a complete unit. On the contrary, in the theory of monism, the two are merged in one. In this case, humans become androgynous, god and devil one divinity, good and evil a coin with two aspects, indistinguishable the one from the other.

According to Plato, in the beginning, male and female were one. As unique beings, they were content and happy; they did not preoccupy themselves with the research of their soul-mate. As a result, they did not sacrifice to the gods and the altars were left cold without any offerings. So Zeus, in a fit of anger and frustration over this lack of respect by the humans, stroke them with his thunder bolt and separated them in men and women. Ever since, humans pray to the gods to help them find and keep their true love. The temples and the altars once again were filled with offerings from the faithful and the aroma of roasting meat filled the air. The priests saw once again their coffers fill up to overflowing.

Is monism to be considered more complete, more autocratic? Do its disciples feel better if they do not have to exchange vows, to whisper love words, to sing love songs, to depend on another person for their happiness? Are humans on the road to simplification, to monism? Who would like this complete perfection, this endless loneliness? Do they think they are on the road to immortality? Or will this road take them directly to eternal mortality?

"No Hermaphrodite for humans", shout men. "No Aphrodite, who needs her, women are useless, only Hermes". "No Hermes, simple Aphrodite will do" cry the women in their turn "men are useless". It seems that the only point on which both sexes agree is that the other sex is useless.

Thankfully, this is an exaggeration. It is a pity that some humans have been so much hurt by the members of the other sex that they have become its sworn and steadfast opponents. Thankfully, most people are still attracted to the other sex. Young people in particular fall in and out of love, and determine their future taking into consideration their love mates. And this is what makes the world go round (still).

Life is in front of us all. Let us not turn our backs to it.

*29 September 2003*
*25 July 2004*
*Glyfada, 20 March 2005*